Navaj

Part 2.

Quest

C. S. Clifford

First published in Great Britain 2017

ISBN: 9 780993 195761

Printed and bound in the UK

A catalogue record of this book is available from the British Library

Edited by Clive Clarke

Cover by Anna E Howlett of Rosehart Studio

THE NAVAJO SERIES
By
C. S. CLIFFORD

Part 1. ACCEPTANCE
ISBN: 9 780993 195754

Part 2. QUEST
ISBN: 9 780993 195761

Part 3. DETOUR
ISBN: 9 780993 195785

Part 4. PENNANCE
ISBN: 9 719993 61143

For more C. S. Clifford Books
visit www.csclifford.co.uk

For Catherine, Niruta and
Pratigya.

Their efforts to become better
writers inspired the first words
of my own writing journey.

And for all those I taught over
the years.

To Cassius
Best Wishes
CSC

Chapter 1:
Yiska's World

Yiska sat at the cliff edge, looking out across the tree canopy that stretched down the mountainside. Only three days' journey from the desert pan, but a place of true beauty and peace. Behind, the mountain continued its upward ascent towards the clouds, and below it fell away, hidden by dense forest.

To the rear of the protruding ledge, where he sat in silent contemplation, huge boulders lay close to the mountain's sheer side, bullying the grace of its lines. Beyond the ledge, and to the right, a rocky outcrop concealed the path that led into the forest.

The boulders behind him hid a secret; a cave within which Yiska lived. The central circular cavern had six short tunnels extending from it like fingers of a starfish. Three formed private spaces for the family members who had cared for him these past years. A fourth stored wood for the fire, while the fifth was for general storage. Water flowed at the rear of the final space, a gift from the spirits. Always fresh, it never ran dry during the summer or froze during the winter. Each of these spaces were closed off with crudely fashioned wooden doors.

The entrance to the cave lacked height and was deep forming a short tunnel, accessed only by stooping low. On one side a second smaller entrance, raised above ground level, was used as a window. The roof of the cave held a narrow hole that led to the outside, allowing smoke from the fire below it to disperse into the atmosphere.

Away from the civilisation of the western world, Yiska had lived contentedly for the past four years. He was now a young adult, six-foot tall, broad at the shoulder and built like an athlete. His long dark hair hung down below his shoulders. Light blue, almost grey, eyes and pale-coloured skin argued with the rest of his facial features, which had Navajo Indian origins; a strong, prominent brow, broad chin and full lips.

The Navajo would describe him as being of mixed spirits: his mother had been a white American, and his father a full-blooded Navajo. Yiska's exact age was unknown as, before coming here, he'd been the victim of an assault from which he'd almost died. He awoke after several days of unconsciousness without memories of life before the assault and worse, with no memory of who he was. Yiska, the name he now used, reflected both his wakening and the lost years. Translated it meant 'the night has passed'.

As he sat, his need dominated his thoughts, to find out about his past, and his origins. He'd waited with consummate patience to come of age, when he could reach out into the western world and seek answers, without fear of being taken into care; no longer deemed a minor in that society.

There was no choice for him and leaving was imminent. Despite the happiness he shared with his adopted family, the questions burned inside him like the fire in a kiln. It was now time to tell them of his plan and it worried him, for his decision would cause them all pain. Even the notion of it brought moisture to his own eyes.

He'd considered telling them while alone with each, but no, in this family they always discussed major decisions, or changes, in a communal setting with each having the right to speak their mind. He wouldn't keep it from them for too much longer, today or tomorrow, it would happen. A special day together before leaving could soften the blow.

Two figures emerged from the cave and came over to join him. They sat close on either side of him; a sign of the intimacy understood and enjoyed by each of them.

"You never tire of that view," the girl said, slipping her arm through his.

"Never! It is the view that pleases me most; it is the land of my home," Yiska replied, a smile on his face as he turned his gaze upon her.

Doli returned his smile, flashing perfect white teeth that contrasted her dark skin so well. Her long black hair mirrored his own but flowed further down her slim figure. Her entrancing eyes were of the deepest blue, the same colour as the bluebird that lived here in Arizona and it was for this that her mother had named her. She was the most beautiful person he'd ever seen, with a personality to match; kind, and considerate. Happiness exuded from her and she showered it on everyone around her with uninhibited abundance.

She broke off a large piece of the flatbread she'd brought from the cave and gave it to him. He bit into it with relish as he spotted bits of dried fruit baked into it, knowing she'd made it especially him, and it tugged at his heart, making his eyes moisten for the second time as he remembered what he was about to reveal.

"This is amazing Doli," he stated, as crumbs stuck to the corners of his mouth. "What fruits have you used this time?"

"That is for me alone," she replied, reaching to address his crumbs. "If I told you all my ways, you would have no further need of me," she told him, adopting a sad look.

7

Yiska feigned shock before replying, "I would still need to feast my eyes on your beauty, Doli."

Her face reddened under her tanned face, but she squeezed his arm in response to the compliment and leaned her head against his shoulder.

"The day is for hunting. We should set traps for rabbits, for they will come out to feed in the sun," Nayati suggested.

Hunting was his favourite task, and he excelled at it. Yiska looked at Doli's twin brother and nodded his agreement. He was as beautiful as his sister, almost identical to her in facial features. Arriving in the world just minutes after his sister, he was as restless as she was calm. Given a name that suited, when translated Nayati meant 'he who wrestles.' He was as tall as Yiska, lean and toned, but towered a good foot above his sister; The two of them shared an unshakable bond over the years they'd lived together, stronger than most natural brothers.

"We should test our skills and hunt in a different place, Brother," Nayati continued.

Yiska recognised a challenge coming and responded before Nayati could continue. "Up the mountain then, ten traps each," he suggested, smiling at Nayati.

"I will hunt too," Doli told them. "I will show you how to do it!"

"You would spend your time more by preparing to cook our catch," Nayati teased.

"If I catch more than you, it should be you to cook tonight," Doli said, raising her eyebrows.

"Now that would be something!" Yiska laughed.

Nayati never could resist a challenge. He gave his sister a scornful glance. "It will be as you say."

"We will pack food, visit the place where we see all and collect the traps on our return," Doli informed them, taking over the preparations and decision-making, as she always did. "And I will ask Grandfather to join the challenge."

Doli entered the cave to make a start, leaving Yiska and Nayati to continue their vigil over the view.

"If she wins the challenge, you'll cook tonight, Nayati?" Yiska asked.

"And if you lose?" Nayati enquired.

"I have only my pride to lose! I did not challenge Doli, because I have learnt that to do so is often to come second best," Yiska replied.

"What you say is true and I should consider more before I speak, but I tell you this; if I cook, it will be the best food you have tasted for a long time," Nayati said.

"That sounds like another challenge to Doli. Be careful, Brother, if you do this you may have to cook more often!"

Yiska laughed at the worry on Nayati's face as he realised, he could end up in a no-win situation.

Doli returned and handed each of them a bundle of snares.

"We will not set the traps until we are high up the mountain," she told them. "I have prepared food, so we can go. Grandfather will not join the hunt, but he will ride Friend and meet us at the place where we see all."

They set off, enjoying the orchestra of sounds in the forest as they travelled up the mountain. The thick canopy above them broke in places allowing sun to illuminate small glades. Trees swayed and creaked gently in the breeze, and birds chirped high on their constant moving branches.

There was no true path to follow here, and they meandered around age-old pine trees, travelling upwards for about an hour before Doli suggested it was time to set the traps. Each sought the best places, looking for droppings, that showed their quarry was near, or the tell-tale signs of runs, the tiny routes the animals often took.

9

Setting their traps, they marked them with fallen branches so that they would recognise them upon their return. Yiska was the least experienced of the three, but he'd watched and practised hard over the past few years. He knew how well his brother hunted, but Doli's skills were so often shrouded by her ability at other tasks. The range of her skills surpassed that of her brother's but some, like hunting, took second place as she took on the responsibility of cleaning and preparing their catch instead. However, her talents would often surprise.

Yiska set his traps carefully but was unconcerned about winning the challenge. Enjoying their time together was his aim, it would be the last hunt with them for a while.

He finished setting his snares last and caught up with the others further up the mountain. A large boulder which seemed out of place in the forest, gave them seating.

"You have taken longer than usual," Nayati told him. "It is so that you worry you will not catch as we do?" he teased."

"I have no such worries, Nayati. I hope you have taken equal care in your preparations and will offer a worthy challenge."

Nayati grinned in response and his diligence at his task was obvious.

"What about you, Doli, have you set with extra care?" Yiska asked.

Doli smiled at him. "I will give my brother something to consider, of this I am sure," she told him. "You also," she added.

"That, I never doubted!" he told her.

They travelled on for another hour before the forest thinned out and they faced the scree at the bottom of yet another mountain. As they walked around its perimeter, they came upon a small clearing with a massive drop-off at the end. No matter how many times he'd seen the view, Yiska never tired of it.

This mighty cliff edge dwarfed the one outside their cave, and the true extent of the canopy below stretched further than the eye could perceive. It rose and fell away on mountain slopes smaller than the one they were standing on. Totally breath-taking! The three of them sat and gazed out absorbing the majesty of the land they lived in.

Chapter 2:
Challenge

A noise from behind drew their attention, announcing Niyol's arrival, the last member of their family. They turned to witness the ancient looking figure mounted upon Friend, a mare that accompanied Niyol for as long as they could remember.

"I see you, Old Man!" Doli greeted him, smiling.

"I see you Doli!" he replied, his voice revealing his pleasure at her smile.

He dismounted and patted the neck of his horse in thanks for the ride.

"Conditions for travel are good, the sun is bright, and the view is clear; I have brought the food that Doli prepared. It is time to eat," he told them, moving to the pack still secured on Friend's back.

Although Niyol was well into his eighties now, his mind was as sharp as ever. He made up for lack of physical prowess by sharing his wealth of knowledge and wisdom with those who now assumed the tasks that life here in the mountains caused. Age lined his face with creases that ran like tributaries in a river delta. Dark brown eyes, hooded by his prominent brow, were bright and clear and held the ability to perceive beyond what was apparent.

Yiska was very fond of the old Navajo who'd saved his life when he found him unconscious in the desert. The old man welcomed him into their home when he regained consciousness and treated him like one of the family from the offset. Mostly, Yiska felt grateful for the identity and lifestyle that Niyol gave him, and often called him 'Teacher' because of the way he taught him about life and the traditional Navajo ways. He honoured all these gifts, striving to show his worthiness of the trust Niyol placed in him, listening carefully to all the old man taught him and adapting to this way of life fully.

After eating, Yiska broke the contented silence they'd been sharing whilst listening to birdsong and the wind in the trees.

"I have been thinking," he started.

Niyol interrupted, continuing for him, "It is time to leave this place to seek answers to the questions in your head"

"You know me well, Teacher?"

"It is easy to see this. Now you are of age, you still cannot find peace here. There is sadness in your face these past weeks as you decide what you need to do. The questions burn like a flame inside you and there is no rest until you have answers. Is this not so?" Niyol asked him.

"It is true, Teacher," Yiska replied and was silent.

A few moments passed before Doli asked, "Will you return to us? When you have found what you need?"

A single tear ran down each of her cheeks. Yiska looked at her, reached out and gently wiped away her tears with his thumbs.

"I will return Doli. I cannot imagine life without your smile to gaze upon and the sound of your laughter to warm me. This is my home, and all of you, my family. No man could wish for more. I will return to you, because it would be impossible to live without you," he told her.

Yiska watched Doli as she stood, walked over to Friend and started stroking her. He felt wretched at the misery he was causing her.

Nayati listened without comment at first, as Yiska would, before smiling with satisfaction at the thoughts that came to him.

"When you go, Brother, it is my thoughts that I will travel with you. You may need help from one who has more experience with his tracking skills. I will see that you do not lose your way and return home safe," he told Yiska.

"You would leave all this to journey with me?" Yiska asked, surprised at his generous offer.

"It is so, I wish to learn of the western world and see what it offers. There are questions I seek answers for. My path in life is yet unknown, but Niyol says we travel many paths. To travel with my brother is the right choice."

"I would be proud to journey with you Brother," Yiska replied.

Niyol listened carefully to the interchange. He was proud of the two young men that sat alongside him; proud of the bond between them the respect they gave each other.

"The words on your tongue are wise, this is good for you Nayati. It will be safer to travel together. Hear my warning Grandsons. The road you follow will bear many branches and each may offer different paths. This can often be the way of shared journeys," he warned. Tell me, Yiska, if you had answers to your questions would you still wish to leave?"

Yiska considered carefully before replying, "If I had the answers, there would be no need for me to leave."

"It is as I thought. You need not leave to seek answers; we discussed this once," Niyol reminded him.

"You mean dream walk, entering the spirit world?" Yiska suggested.

"Yes. If you agree to this, I will stay by your side and help with your return," Niyol said.

"You also said that this could be dangerous, that sometimes when people enter the spirit world they do not return," Yiska replied.

"This is true, but you are older and stronger, and I can help you," Niyol stated.

"It is worth a try." Yiska told him.

They let the subject drop and returned to the silence they all found comfort in. Doli returned from Friend and sat close to Yiska, unable to hide the sadness in her face.

Soon Niyol suggested they head back down the mountain to seek the results of the competition.

"Many seasons have passed since you cooked Nayati!" he teased, trying to lighten the sombre mood.

"I am thinking that more seasons will pass before this is so," Nayati said, confident in his ability to hunt.

"You are too sure Brother," said Doli, forcing a smile.

As they approached the area, they separated to locate the markers for their own traps. Yiska was unsuccessful, but Nayati and Doli each caught a rabbit.

They returned to where Niyol sat waiting for them, Doli and Nayati both hiding their catch behind their backs. Yiska was empty-handed.

"You have no catch, Brother! How do you explain this?" asked Nayati, feigning a stern voice.

Yiska held up his hands in an open gesture with resignation on his face. "How many did you get?" he asked.

Nayati presented his single catch with a huge grin.

"Doli can you remove the grin from Nayati's face?" asked Yiska, his eyes widened in expectation.

She revealed her catch.

"We each have one rabbit, yet you have none, Yiska," Nayati laughed.

"The competition is unfinished, Brother, for I did not bet for cooking. Let me look at your rabbits!" Yiska held them up, side by side and considered them. "Hmm Niyol, Doli's rabbit is bigger and heavier than Nayati's. Because of this, Doli wins."

The grin disappeared from Nayati's face, causing Niyol to laugh out loud. "I remember no talk about size," Nayati commented, looking dismayed. "But as my brother gives Doli the win, I shall accept defeat, as this is rare, and I will cook a meal that each of you will remember for many moons."

Doli looked delighted and slipped her arm through Yiska's.

Nayati kept his word and produced an excellent meal for them all. Niyol suggested that he should cook while Doli took care of the hunting, and both smiled at the intended compliments. Yiska moved outside while Doli cleared away the remains of their meal. The sun was setting over the canopy below leaving streaks of pink, red, orange and mauve. Horizontal flames across the sky. It was beautiful, each colour deepening as the sun dropped lower. He became aware of the old man's presence beside him, even though his arrival was silent.

"It will be another good day tomorrow," Niyol announced, with the certainty of one who'd seen thousands of sunsets such as this. "As we journeyed home today, I collected the roots we need, that you may enter the world of the spirits," he told Yiska. "I am thinking that should be soon, perhaps tomorrow."

"The sooner the better," replied Yiska.

"There is much for you to learn; we will talk more when we rise," Niyol added.

Yiska nodded his agreement and together, they stood quietly, watching the sun disappear from the sky.

Chapter 3:
Preparations

As the sun rose, Yiska left his sleeping mat and walked outside. A restless night, his mind had been full of worry and uncertainty for both the dream walk and his impending departure. Although he respected the Navajo beliefs, some areas of their culture were more difficult to embrace than others. He doubted the dream walk would provide him with the information he sought, thus making the delay pointless.

His thoughts dwelled on the loss he would impose upon Doli and Niyol when he left, and the loss that he would sense too. They were all so close and their lives had become intricately woven together.

Cursing his lack of memories, he wondered, for the millionth time, how he knew so much, yet had no recollection of his identity or life before the assault?

Although Niyol had not yet discussed details of the dream walk, Yiska was apprehensive, even fearful. When the spirits returned memories in the past, the experience had been painful and raised more unanswered questions. He was safe in Niyol's hands, he knew that, the old man loved him like a grandson.

Trying to block out the deluge of negativity in his mind, Yiska looked up, seeing the eagle flying its circular path high above him, and the sight brought comfort to his troubled mind. His spirit animal had not left him since his discovery in the desert years before. Several times now, it had warned him of impending danger and even saved his life from a deadly rattlesnake once.

The great bird was also Nayati's and Doli's animal spirit and he wondered whether it would follow him when he left or stay with Doli. He wanted the protection the bird offered to remain with her.

His previous, more negative thoughts returned and his head was in such turmoil that he walked into the forest to subdue it. After a few minutes, when he still hadn't found peace, he began to run. The pounding of his feet settled into a rhythmical pace and he felt the tension diminishing as his distance from the cave increased. He ran for several miles, before stopping in a small glade where a profusion of spring flowers had caught his attention. Picking a selection for Doli, he returned to the cave at a much slower pace.

His family were all about their duties and Doli looked up and smiled as he offered her the flowers. She selected a bright red one, shortened its stem and placed it in her hair just above her ear. Then she found a narrow container for the rest, arranging them in a manner that pleased her and stood them by the window.

Niyol moved toward him and suggested that they attend Friend together and Yiska knew instinctively that he wanted to talk to him alone. He followed the old man into the forest, to a shelter constructed for Friend.

From three sides, the structure appeared to be a large bush, but access on the fourth revealed the inside. Vertical branches, driven into the ground formed the main structure of the sides and rear, with others tied across the top to form a roof. Thinner, flexible branches, with their foliage intact, were interwoven between them, resulting in a strong structure that offered the mare protection from the elements. Every year some of the branches took root whilst

Niyol replaced those that didn't to maintain it. A second structure, built to one side, offered storage for wood, hay, straw and the litter that Friend dragged when they needed transportation.

Niyol brushed down the mare using a twig brush, whilst Yiska replaced the soiled straw with fresh. Next he tied a bundle of hay to the side of the structure. Without a door to the shelter, the horse could come and go as she pleased. Remarkably, Friend was nearly always there, or was close enough to return at the sound of Niyol's whistle when needed. They had been together for more than twenty years now and had a companionship based on trust and affection.

After he'd finished their tasks, Niyol suggested they walk to some of their gardens. In the forest there were small clearings, allowing sunlight through; they had cultivated several of these to grow a variety of vegetables and wheat. They sowed randomly to disguise their industry and allowed weeds and wildflowers to compete naturally with their crop to further conceal it. The soil in the mountain forest was poor, and their success was limited, which was why they had several gardens scattered over a larger area.

"It will be time to clear the ground and scatter seed soon," Niyol stated. "It would be good to do this before you leave," he added.

"I would be happy to help with this," Yiska told him. Niyol led Yiska to a fallen tree and beckoned him to sit down.

"I will explain the dream walk ritual to you, to ease your concerns," Niyol said.

"No harm will come to me whilst you are with me, Teacher," Yiska replied, trying to hide his worries.

"The dream walk is not without risk. How much of the root needed to enter the spirit world is different with each man. To eat too much may cause sickness; it is said that the spirits keep some people, leaving their bodies without life."

Yiska squirmed a little, unable to hide the doubts forming in his mind.

"The visit does not promise answers, the spirits reveal only what they wish to reveal," Niyol continued.

"If I do not get answers from the spirits, then I will search for them myself. It eats away at me," Yiska told him.

"This I understand, Yiska, and I will help you find your way, but know what I say is true. You are Yiska of the Navajo. You are the person I have known since the day I found you. It was a good day! Your home and family are here and will remain so for all time."

"I know Teacher, I'm happy here. I will continue to honour all the things you've taught me and even after I find the answers I seek, I will return as Yiska of the Navajo," Yiska said emphatically.

"We must return, and make ready for tonight," Niyol stated.

Later that day Niyol erected a small camping tepee on the clearing in front of the cave. They used this for shelter when they hunted during the winter months. He placed some small rocks in a circle in front of this and collected wood ready for a fire. He then disappeared into the cave to grind and prepare the roots that Yiska would take.

Yiska followed him to ask more about the ritual.

"You must not eat before; this way you will need less of the roots," he explained.

"What will happen to me? I mean, what will I experience?" Yiska asked nervously.

"You must breathe in the scent of the roots. It will appear you float on water. Then you will chew the roots. You must swallow the juices only, not the root itself. Where you walk in the spirit world is unknown, but when you wake, it will be as a dream. With the spirits' help, you will have your answers."

20

"And if I don't wake?" asked Yiska, in a quieter voice.

"I will be here to see you wake," Niyol said confidently.

That evening, as soon as it was completely dark, Niyol led Yiska out of the cave to the tepee and told him to sit. Doli and Nayati remained in the cave. Niyol placed the bowl with the crushed roots to heat in front of the fire and then started to chant in the Athabaskan language of the Navajo. Yiska listened to the melody and began to relax slightly, despite the nervousness he was experiencing. On and on Niyol chanted and, as the mixture heated, the vapours from it curled upwards for Yiska to breathe in.

At first, the odour turned his nose, but he forced himself to inhale as Niyol had instructed him. His body calmed, and the scent became more acceptable. deeper and deeper he relaxed, Niyol's chanting became distant, and he did not respond when the old man asked him to chew the roots that were ready. He hardly felt Niyol place them inside his mouth, but started to chew, swallowing the juices that flooded his mouth when he did so.

Niyol observed carefully to ensure that Yiska did not swallow the roots and continued to do so as the young man's head slipped forward towards his knees. He gently removed the remnants of the root from his mouth and pushed him down until he was lying on his side.

"Dream well, Yiska, seek your answers, and allow the spirits to guide you," he whispered, and sat down beside him to keep vigil.

Niyol expected Yiska to stay in the dream world for as long as two days and nights. He had brought water with him but had no need or desire to leave Yiska alone. He had asked Nayati to bring him food in the morning at their normal time but advised him not to venture out of the cave while the spirits were so close.

It would be impossible to relieve Nayati and Doli of their worries and concerns for Yiska, but his reassurance came from the knowledge that they had each other to share the burden.

As he sat, he contemplated the implications of Yiska leaving the mountain. Niyol would miss Yiska terribly, as would his granddaughter. He admired the way Yiska prepared to face his demons and his gentle nature, especially after being treated so badly by those who had attacked him.

He also admired his intelligence, the manner in which he learnt so quickly, and offered suggestions to improve the things they'd taught him. Most of all, Niyol would miss the quiet companionship they shared, the way Yiska never spoke unless he had something worthwhile to say. He may not leave yet, thought Niyol, but with no real conviction. His thoughts continued as he sat quietly alongside his ward, until Yiska started to moan from deep inside.

Chapter 4:
Dream Walk

Yiska's body seemed light, as if floating on a lake, it was difficult to move and control it. His mind wandered, unable to focus, yet he was indifferent to what was happening to him. He did not feel Niyol place the roots in his mouth and wasn't even aware that he began to chew them. Swallowing the fluid, resulting from mastication, he lost all awareness as the it acted upon his body and mind; his eyes closed, and blackness engulfed him.

For a short while there was nothing, but gradually an image started to form. Looking down, from a great height, he saw his home spinning unaware of the words he cried, but the call of an eagle swallowed the sound he'd made. Still circling the space above his home, with a conscious effort, he forced himself downwards. He descended slowly but did not stop as he approached the cave. This time he was heading for the sloping rock above the cave entrance that connected it to the more vertical rock of the mountainside. Realising he would impact it, he braced himself for the shock, but his vision became masked with blackness and he passed through the rock instead.

Inside the cave, he looked around at the familiar surroundings, not questioning what he'd just experienced.

Everything appeared as it should, except for something different about the doors to the six chambers leading from the central area. At first, he couldn't discern what the difference was but, as he examined the doors, a locked padlock barred entry on each one. He looked at them with confusion. There are no locks, he told himself. We have no need of them. He called out for Niyol, but again the cry of an eagle drowned his voice.

It was then that he found six keys on the table in the living area and reached out to take one. Placing it into the padlock on the first of the doors, he turned it. The internal mechanism clicked as it released its grip on the clasp and he removed it from the door.

Inside a large familiar room, something else was amiss, though he didn't know what. The space was vast! There were two rows of four beds, each flanked by a cupboard with drawers on one side.

A young boy entered the room and sat on a bed, oblivious to his presence. He watched him take a small key from a length of string tied around his neck and open the top drawer. The boy withdrew a small wooden box with two gold coloured inlaid lines following the perimeter of the lid. He opened it and tipped the contents out onto the grey blanket covering the bed.

Yiska watched as the boy put a silver St Christopher on a chain over his head. He then looked wistfully at three photographs, studying them carefully. Next he picked up two tarnished medals, attached to short pieces of ribbon. Not spending much time on those, he put them back onto the bed and moved quickly on to the last item, a letter. He removed it from the envelope and looked at it, turning it this way and that, squinting his eyes as he did so. Yiska looked at it too. The beautiful italic writing seemed to dance on the page and meant little to him.

He continued observing as the boy collected up his things and put them back into the box. Placing it back into the drawer, he locked it before tucking the key carefully back inside his shirt. Then he left the room. Yiska waited until the room darkened before leaving it and shutting the door behind him.

Back at the table, he selected another key, opened the lock to the next room, and moved inside.

The boy was there again, older now; a teenager. He sat on the bed, once more examining the contents from his box and Yiska saw the care with which he replaced each item in it. They were precious to him. Again, the boy returned the box to the drawer and locked it.

A familiar, but distant voice, drew his attention. "I want that box and all the things inside it."

A silhouette of a larger person loomed, but the features were vague and frightening because of it.

The boy replied, "You can't have it; it's mine, not yours."

Yiska recognised the fear in the boy's face and the trembling of his lips. Then the room darkened suddenly, and everything disappeared from view, so Yiska retreated, shutting the door behind him.

He selected another key from the table and turned it in the lock of the next door. It seemed to turn in the lock on its volition and the padlock fell from the hasp; he entered the room.

The boy was there again on his bed with a frightened look on his face as the same silhouette moved towards him.

A youth of about eighteen materialised from the shadows. He had a long scar beneath his lower lip, a nose flattened from multiple breaks and small, menacing eyes. Two smaller figures followed him, giggling at the boy's fear.

Yiska caught his breath as the youth smashed a blow into the boy's face with a clenched fist. The other two assailants held the boy down whilst the older one wrenched the key from his neck and removed the box from the drawer.

25

They struck the boy again before being releasing him, and the youths walked away casually, laughing again.

The boy followed his attackers out to an old truck, climbing over the tailgate into the back. He remained, concealed as it drove into the desert, where the youths parked and built a campfire a short distance away.

Night was drawing in, and the three of them sat around it drinking beer; the older boy sitting with the box in his hands. They threw their empty bottles against the rocks and laughed as they smashed. As soon as they had fallen asleep, the boy left the truck and walked quietly towards the campsite. He took the box carefully from the leader and started to retreat, but his foot stepped onto a shard of glass with a loud crunching sound. Instantly, the leader woke and grabbed his hand.

"What have we here?" he drawled. He reached out to grab the box back, but the younger boy held on to it.

Yiska felt anger as the boy received a punch hard in the face and was then kicked repeatedly as he fell to the ground. The other two joined in, raining blow after blow until the boy stopped moving. The leader ordered the others to place him in the truck, saying that they would dump him in the desert. Again, the room darkened and Yiska left, shutting the door behind.

Yiska grabbed another key and tried the next padlock. It opened easily. Pushing open the door, he entered a different room, which appeared to be the main living area of a small house. It was lit by a single candle and Yiska saw a tired-looking, young woman sitting on an old, threadbare armchair. He recognised her from the photographs in the box. She was talking to a child, about four years old, sitting on her lap.

"So, we don't have any choice. You must go where there is somebody to take care of you properly," she told the child.

"But I don't want to go without you," the child said, burying his head against her.

"I know, darling, but we must be brave."

Tears ran down both faces and Yiska felt his own fall down onto his cheeks, then the room darkened.

Yiska left and closed the door. He offered one of the two remaining keys to the lock and the eagle cried out again and again, so loudly, that it forced him to cover his ears. As he moved his hand away from the lock to do this, the cries stopped. Repeating his actions, the same thing happened, this time louder still. He returned the key and exchanged it for the last one and walked to the last door. Again, he offered the key to the lock, but the eagle's cries returned and did not stop until he moved away from it.

As he replaced it on the table he started to rise. He lifted a hand to protect his head from the ceiling, but no impact came as he passed through the rock. Below, he watched as the cave become gradually smaller and rotate as before. He called out for Niyol, but the cry of the eagle drowned out the sound of his voice. This time the entire world around him darkened, and he lost awareness as his senses started to fade too.

"It is time to wake, Yiska," said a familiar voice inside his head. "It is time to wake."

Yiska opened his eyes. As he started to focus, Niyol's voice became clearer.

"Good, you have returned to us! How do you feel?"

"Thirsty," Yiska replied. "Very thirsty!"

Niyol passed him a cup of water, refilling it for him the moment it was empty. "Do you have pain, Yiska?"

"No, though I do feel a little sick," he replied.

"This is normal. Rest, and it will pass."

Seeing familiar surroundings around him, he realised he was back in the cave.

"How long has it been?"

"The sun has set and risen twice," replied Niyol.

"Two days! It seemed so much shorter," he said, surprised.

"It is the way. It is still dark outside, sleep a while and we will talk again when you wake," Niyol instructed.

Yiska closed his eyes and fell asleep almost immediately. This time there were no dreams!

Chapter 5:
Decisions

When Yiska woke again, he lay quiet, watching Doli prepare their morning meal. She sensed his gaze and smiled as their eyes met.

"You slept long," she whispered. "You are better?"

"Much better than when I first woke," he replied, sitting up.

"You are hungry?" she asked.

"I'm always hungry for your cooking," he answered with a glint in his eye.

Doli blushed before she presented him with a bowl of wheat porridge. He wolfed it and thanked her before raising himself slowly and walking outside.

Niyol and Nayati were sitting in their favourite place at the drop-off overlooking the forest canopy.

"You are well Brother?" asked Nayati.

"Yes," replied Yiska, squeezing in between them.

The two men refrained from asking about his dream-walk with the time-honoured patience of the Navajo, but Yiska knew that they wanted to know, and he did not wish to keep them waiting.

"Doli has food for you," he told them, "and after that I will tell you what I experienced."

"Then we must eat for I hunger more than usual," Niyol said, rising from his sitting position.

Nayati stood too and followed him into the cave.

Yiska smiled to himself, knowing the way Niyol had disguised what he had wanted. They returned after they had eaten, with Doli at their side. Sitting close in a small circle, they looked at Yiska waiting for him to begin.

He told them the details leading up to the fourth door and paused, "Tell me what you make of this so far Teacher," Yiska invited.

"Each door hides a different memory. I believe that you were one with the spirit eagle, for you tell your story as the eagle that even now flies above us."

They all looked up to see the sight that they had become so accustomed to seeing, before Niyol continued.

"When you called for me, the eagle cry took away your voice. The eagle cry was your voice!"

He refrained from further comment, waiting for Yiska to continue.

Yiska told them about the fourth room, again asking for Niyol's input.

"The woman was your mother, and you the small child. It is a painful memory for she says that she could no longer care for you."

"That is how I understood it too. But why?" he asked, the misery in his voice clear.

"Few things would make a mother give up her child. Her reasons are powerful, the spirits did not reveal all."

"The spirits are not ready to release more memories," Niyol stated, after Yiska had finished telling them the rest of his dream-walk,

Yiska looked disappointed, "I've waited for so long to get my memory back. If the spirits won't help me, then I must find the answers for myself. I need to know."

"When will you leave?" Niyol asked him.

"In a few days."

"I will go with you, Brother," Nayati said calmly. "I wish to know how others live. There is much to see and learn.

It will be safer if we travel together. When we find answers, we will return."

"You honour me Nayati, because you wouldn't be going if I weren't. How long this journey will take is unknown, but you're right, we will return!" Yiska said.

Doli listened to this exchange without contributing and tears fell down her cheeks; life on the mountain without the two young men, so much a part of her existence, would change everything.

Niyol looked up as an idea occurred to him.

"We will travel down the mountain with you. It is time for the spring market; I will trade with my granddaughter this year," he said.

Doli did not respond, but her silent tears continued to flow unchecked.

"We must make ready for the journey. It is right to prepare today," Niyol added.

They rose from their seat to gather and pack the things they had made for trade during the long winter months. Yiska put his arm round Doli's shoulders, as they walked the short distance back to the cave, and she smiled though her heart weighed heavy.

"I was not expecting Nayati's company on my journey Niyol; The sowing of the spring seeds?"

"Doli and I will attend to this when we return from trading. A few days will make little difference," he replied. "It is my knowing that parting is more difficult if delayed."

A short while later, a pile of goods for trade had accumulated outside the cave and Niyol asked Yiska to take it to the wood store in the forest. He told him to load it onto the litter that they stored there and then suggested that Doli assisted him. They selected the cured furs from the animals

31

they had hunted during the winter months first, as these were the bulkiest. Loaded onto the litter in several bundles, the gaps between where used for smaller goods.

They walked side by side, in silence, until they reached the wood store. Yiska put down his load and pulled out the litter. It comprised two wooden poles about ten feet long and a few inches in diameter. Held at one end by a leather harness to Friend's shoulders, the opposite end would drag on the ground. The three cross struts, about three-foot long, were carved out at the ends to sit between the poles which were then secured with lengths of twisted sinew. Four deer hides formed the base of the litter and laced with sinew.

Doli started to load the furs, spreading the weight on the litter. They left these unsecured for the moment. Yiska was about to return to the cave when Doli stopped him.

"It is so that I do not wish you to leave Yiska. Can you not find peace here with life?" she asked him.

"I wish I could, Doli, but the questions invade my thoughts every day. Everything here is right, except what I don't know."

Doli's shoulders slumped, and she fell silent. Yiska was unsure what to say, and both continued with their task.

A selection of baskets and containers that Doli had weaved followed the furs, then wooden carvings that the three men had spent hours shaping. Clothing and moccasins that Doli had made from buckskin. Plenty to trade for, to make life here easier.

After their evening meal, Niyol wandered into his private space. Yiska had only known him to do this a couple of times in all the time he had stayed with them and had assumed that he kept little inside it. When he returned, he was carrying a bundle.

"I have been thinking of what you will need when you leave here," he said to Nayati and Yiska. "The ways of others are different to ours."

He put down the bundle and picked out western denims and shirts for them.

Nayati looked at them with such disgust that Doli laughed. He had worn them before; several times at trading markets and hated them.

"There are no shoes to give you," Niyol continued, "but many wear the moccasins we use"

He also gave them two worn knapsacks that were approaching twenty years old, telling them that they once belonged to his daughter and her husband.

"They used these when they walked for pleasure, to carry food for the day."

Then he showed them a bundle of money. "For many years I have carried this," he told them. "I take this when we trade, for we might not get all we need, but never have I used it. In the western world they use it for all you need. Hide it well; it attracts bad people if seen in such amounts. It may be difficult to find a place to stay; if you do, you will need money to pay for it."

Yiska took it, recognising several of the bills and knowing that there was a substantial amount in his hands.

Then Niyol gave Nayati a small carving of an eagle, similar to the one that Nayati had made and given to Yiska when he had first come to the cave.

"Keep this with you for protection," his face solemn, before suggesting that Yiska take his too. "Keep your knives in your bags too. The western people do not wear these as we do," he warned.

"You are wise, Old Man; I hear your words," Nayati told him.

"We will take care of each other," Yiska assured him, sensing the old man's concern. Then he changed the subject.

"What will Doli wear when she goes to the market with you?"

"She will dress like western girls," Niyol replied.

He moved back into his private space, emerging with a neat cloth bundle. Unfolding it, he held it up. The dress was white and sprinkled with small red flowers.

"It would be good to see you wear this, Doli, for you are as beautiful as your mother when she first wore it."

Doli took it and held it against her face, experiencing its softness.

"My mother's?" she asked, her eyes wide with surprise and then pleasure. Niyol nodded.

She disappeared into the water room to try on the new dress. A few minutes later, she ran back into the cave, smoothing down the dress with her hands. Yiska and Nayati gazed at her in disbelief.

"Why do you stare at me?" she asked, a little worried. "Do I look strange?"

Yiska paused before answering, "I've never seen you look so beautiful!"

Nayati nodded his agreement. "It is my thinking he will remember you like this while we journey," he told Doli with a smile.

"It is like your mother breathes again," said Niyol, and she beamed at his compliment.

Doli disappeared to take off the dress and Yiska spoke in a quiet voice.

"I will leave soon Niyol if you agree?"

"Everything is prepared; we can leave in the morning," Niyol answered.

"I would like a day alone with Doli before I leave. I will take her into the forest for a picnic; do something nice for her."

"She would like this. Nayati and I will scatter some seed while you do this. Have you told her?"

"I want it to be a surprise."

"Nayati and I will not talk of this, but I will say we will travel after tomorrow."

"Thank you."

34

Chapter 6:
A Private Goodbye

The following morning Yiska left his sleeping mat well before the break of dawn and started to prepare some food for him and Doli to take with them. Making breakfast and willow bark tea for them all, he passed Nayati a cup as soon as he stirred.

"It is my thoughts that you are still doing the work of women Brother," Nayati told him sternly, but with amusement clear in his eyes.

Yiska opened his mouth to reply but Nayati spoke again.

"I see what you have done for Doli and understand the reasons for this. I learned this from you long ago when you first came here. She will like the way you honour her."

Yiska grinned at him, "That is my intention."

Niyol woke next and Yiska passed him some tea.

"This is as good as Doli makes," he said, sipping the hot liquid.

"Doli taught me how to. I thought it would be good if we drank this and watched the sunrise together."

"It shall be as you say, the weather is kind and each man should respect the rising and falling of the sun."

Doli stirred at the sound of their voices and Yiska passed her drink across.

She thanked Yiska who smiled at her warmly and then left the cave with Nayati and Niyol following.

"You are quick to leave when food is ready," she said, with an air of curiosity as she followed them out. "I am right that Yiska made this also?"

"It is as you say Granddaughter, but the food can wait for we will thank the spirits for the rising of the sun."

Niyol and Nayati sat either side of Yiska and Doli remained standing.

"Grandfather you will move for me to sit next to the man who honours me by doing the tasks that I would do each day?"

"I will, for that means that you will sit next to me also," Niyol replied giving her a smile.

The lightening sky was already starting to turn pink on the distant horizon and, as they watched, a tiny crimson arc burst above it and instantly started to grow. Even that first glimpse radiated a glowing warmth that each of them felt, and they sat in silence until the sun had revealed its entirety.

"Time to eat," Niyol said, rising and making his way back to the cave with the others close behind.

After they devoured the meal, Doli started to collect the dirty dishes when Niyol stopped her.

"Yiska prepared food so that you and he might spend time together. Nayati and I will clean these."

"It is as Grandfather says," Nayati added taking the dish from her.

Doli's mouth dropped open in surprise. Yiska often did things for her but this was a Nayati she rarely witnessed.

"I have trained our brother in the ways of women Doli and he understands the need to practise," Yiska said in a solemn tone.

"You will leave now Brother, or I will wash you also," Nayati said, in the same solemn manner as Yiska.

36

Doli and Niyol laughed at the exchange and Yiska picked up the bundle he had packed for the day. He took Doli's hand and led her from the cave. For a long while they said nothing and just enjoyed the time on their own but Doli's natural inquisitiveness forced her to question.

"Where are we going Yiska?"

"We are visiting places that have special meaning to me."

"What places?"

"You will know when we arrive."

"We could collect herbs while we walk."

"Not today."

"But we will pass what we need?"

"Today is for fun, not work."

"It is so, that you told me it is good to do both."

"I did, didn't I, and can you remember the place where I said this?"

"I remember you explaining what a picnic was. We were sitting on a fallen tree in a small clearing after collecting some plants for healing."

"Does this place look familiar then?" he asked, as they rounded an old pine and entered a small clearing.

"This is the place. How is it that you remember this?"

"I remember this because I taught you how to have fun. Do you remember what we did?"

"That is easy, for I remember it as the tea you made this morning."

Releasing his hand, she lay down on a patch of grass.

"The clouds are almost still; I would share this with you now, as we did long ago."

Yiska grinned and lay down beside her and they spent a while exploring images in the clouds that existed more in their imagination than the clouds themselves. Before long Yiska stood and held out his hand to help her up and the two of them travelled further into the forest. He stopped at an old pine that had stood longer than the rest of the surrounding trees, judging by its thickness.

"You showed me something here that I'd never seen before. Can you remember what?"

At first Doli looked a little puzzled but as she walked round the trunk of the pine, she saw the mark that Yiska had made four years ago. She suddenly smiled and fluttered her eyelids to catch his attention.

"This is Bluebird Tree; you named it when I showed you the bird whose name, they gave me. The colour of my eyes and the bird show my name is right with me. This mark, you made with the knife that Niyol gave you."

Yiska took her hand grinning and led her away. After another half an hour of walking, he stopped at an incline and walked halfway up.

"And this place?"

Doli looked around beaming. "This is the place of the snowstorm. We made a cave in the snow for shelter. My hands were so cold, and you saved them from the black sickness that eats fingers and toes."

"What else do you remember?"

"This is the place where you kissed me for the first time," she answered coyly.

Yiska placed his hand on the small of her back and pulled her towards him and with his other hand he lifted her chin and kissed her as gently as he had the first time. When their lips parted, he held her tight against him and she lay her head on his chest.

"There are few times to share the closeness with you Yiska and now as you leave there will be none," she whispered gently.

Yiska heard the misery in her whisper. "We will make more time for this when I return, I promise you."

Doli made no attempt to answer or move from the embrace. They stood, locked together, long enough for the sun to have risen higher the sky. Then they ate their picnic before spending the afternoon finding more places of significance to them both.

The day passed far too quick and soon the sun was lowering gracefully towards the horizon. As they turned homeward, about a mile from their cave, Doli stopped.

"The sun will not shine on me after you leave Yiska. It will know that my heart is sad, and that it cannot make me smile."

"When the sadness is at its worst, visit a place we've come to today and remember what happened. Every time I visit these places I always smile at the memories and you will too. I have something to leave with you while I am gone."

He opened the pack that had carried the food and took out something small, concealed in his grasp. He took her hand and placed it in her palm.

"Yiska it is beautiful, each part is true to the bird," she exclaimed, with a mixture of surprise and pleasure.

She was accurate in her description and the little wooden Bluebird was the best carving Yiska had ever done.

"Grandfather will know the patience the work took," she added.

"I am glad that you like it Doli."

"This is already my favourite thing. I will give you something of me to travel with when we are home."

Yiska smiled and kissed her again before leading her back to the cave.

They arrived just as the sun was setting. Niyol and Nayati were watching, sitting together at the drop off.

"Old Man see what Yiska has made for me," Doli said excitedly, forgetting to greet him in her normal way.

"What is it that distracts you from the hug that I am used to getting from you?"

"This Grandfather," she said, passing over the carving.

"It pleasures me to see the work that has gone into carving this Yiska. I could not carve better. Look at this Nayati and judge your brother's skill."

"My thinking is that Yiska has traded for this at a past market. It cannot be that he carves better than his brother who has practised for many more years than him."

Yiska grinned at the compliment and passed it back to Doli who clasped it tightly before taking it inside. She called Yiska to her.

"When Nayati went to his first trade market he came back with a necklace for me. I did not go, for you slept with the spirits. The necklace is special, and I make some for the market. This one is for you Yiska."

She passed it over, and he looked at the alternate coloured wooden beads that hung from a length of sinew. The brown beads were circular and the black ones cylindrical. She took it back before he could comment, placed it around his neck and tied the two ends.

"You will not forget me after you leave."

"I could never forget you Doli. Thank you, it is beautiful."

"I keep something of you, and you keep something of me. The journey moves us apart, it is right to have such things."

Chapter 7:
Parting

Soon after dawn, and once they had covered the entrance to the cave in rocks, they made their way to the wood store to collect Friend and the litter.

Before long they were travelling down the mountain, as they had done many times before. They journeyed in silence, each thinking of the parting that would soon take place, uncertain of how long it would be until they were together again, and aware of the potential disruption to their dependable, interwoven lives.

They ate on the move, not intending to stop until they reached the campsite that Niyol and Nayati had used before. Arriving as the sun was setting, Nayati lit a small fire, Doli prepared food and Niyol and Yiska sat down together a little way off.

"I will ask something of you," Niyol said, a concerned expression on his face. "You have knowledge of the western world. I worry that Nayati will not find their ways easy to understand; he may become…" He paused, searching for the right word… troubled. I ask that you stay close and help him learn, so that he gains knowledge that he may need later in life."

Yiska nodded, "he is my brother."

"It is as you say," Niyol replied, satisfied.

On the morning of the second day's travel the mood was sombre as they ate a small, silent breakfast before breaking camp. The plan was to descend further down the mountain and travel along its outer edge. There was little cover, but safety came with the knowledge that few people passed that way.

As they skirted the fringe of the desert, Niyol indicated towards the area where he had found Yiska four years ago. It was some distance off their route, and Yiska was reluctant to return to the place where his assailants had dumped him to die, so the group continued their journey.

At noon, they reached a sheltered but rocky area a few miles south of Mason, and it was here that Niyol suggested Yiska and Nayati hide the things they would not need whilst in town. He helped them find a small clearing amongst the rocks and there they concealed the few possessions they had brought. Then the group continued on towards Mason. After a while, Niyol stopped and announced that he and Doli would turn off to head for the market grounds. He pointed out the dust track ahead that led into town and told the two young men to follow that. The parting they all dreaded had arrived.

"Journey well and be safe," Niyol told Nayati. "Seek your answers and return to us," he told Yiska. They hugged as if it was for the last time. Doli declined to say anything, but tears rolled down her face as she embraced first her brother and then Yiska.

"Come Doli," Niyol ordered and walked away.

She followed leaving Nayati and Yiska alone. They stood and watched as Niyol and Doli travelled on. Yiska waited for her to turn, hoping for one more glimpse at her beautiful face. She didn't, but he continued staring until they disappeared in the heat haze, his fingers rubbing the beads on the necklace she had made for him and unable to check the tears that fell from his own eyes.

"It is time to go Brother," said Nayati. "She will be home when we return."

The two of them strode out along the track and followed it into the town. They approached a large sign at the side of the track that said, 'Welcome to Mason - population 6024.'

Nayati looked at it and asked Yiska what it said, but Yiska couldn't read it either; the lettering danced around on the board. They continued on and the town started to appear through the heat haze.

"It is strange that people live in these buildings," Nayati said as they passed brick and wooden dwellings.

"They would think us strange too if they saw our cave," Yiska replied.

"They live close to their neighbours and there is little space," Nayati continued.

"It is what they are used to," Yiska told him.

"This is not for me, Yiska."

"You are lucky Nayati, because you don't have to," Yiska said, smiling at his brother's disgust.

Up ahead he saw a group of children playing in a fenced off area. As they approached, there was an athletics track, bordered along the straights with small seating areas.

"What is this place?" Nayati asked.

Yiska explained.

"Why do they run in circles? They do not go anywhere! What is the point?" he asked, confused.

To his amusement Yiska explained the concept of sport and the personal challenge that the sport offered.

"Why do we sometimes challenge each other to races or in hunting?" Yiska asked him.

"We do this to show who is best and sometimes, it is because we can," Nayati responded, starting to understand.

"Right! they do it their way," Yiska told him.

"I would stay and watch a while," Nayati told him and walked to the seating area to sit down.

Yiska saw that a priest was organising the sporting events. Short and balding he had a pleasant, almost serene face, and was busy dividing a large group of children, ranging in age from about eleven to eighteen, into teams of four.

"Looks like he's organising a relay race," Yiska said, and explained the idea to Nayati.

The teams lined up in order of size, smallest first and the race started. The team closest to them were cruising on the first lap, but as they broke lanes on the second, both were in contention to win.

Nayati looked at the older boys waiting for their chance to run and commented to Yiska that they did not look like runners. "They are too thin, no muscles in their legs," he said.

"It's deceiving, Nayati, they're distance runners," Yiska told him. They watched the race unfold as the last runners took their turn and they surprised Nayati at the speed they built up.

"You are right, Brother," Nayati said to Yiska when the race had finished, and as the runners bent down, holding on to their knees to get their breath back. "They ran at speed but seemed tired by the end of the circle. They would do better to start out at a slower pace, perhaps."

He turned his attention to the priest. "He wears the clothes of a woman?"

Yiska laughed. "They are not women's clothes; they are the clothes of a priest," he replied.

"And what is a priest?"

"A person who communicates with, and works for God, to encourage people to live in God's way. I suppose in Navajo terms he is one who communicates with the spirit world, but in his eyes, there is only one spirit, called God," Yiska explained.

"Only one spirit?" asked Nayati incredulously.

"Yes! A powerful spirit who created everything. The people give thanks to him in places called churches, usually on a Sunday, but they can do it whenever they need."

"It is strange, we do not need such places."

"Just different," explained Yiska.

Their conversation had blinkered them from the rest of the world, and they hadn't seen the priest approach them before his voice caught their attention.

"Hi there, boys, I'm Father Michael. I don't suppose either of you are runners, are you? We've an athletics meet with Muirfield next week and it sure would be good if we had extra runners." He held out his hand.

Yiska took it, surprised at the strength of his grip.

"I am Yiska and this is my brother, Nayati."

"Navajo names eh?" he enquired, grabbing Nayati's hand in the same vice-like grip.

"I am Nayati of the Navajo," Nayati said. "You have knowledge of the Navajo?" he asked.

"Plenty of people here connected to the Navajo. I learn more about them the longer I live here," Father Michael grinned.

"How long have you been here?" Yiska asked.

"Only about four years," he replied. "What about you two? I've not seen you around before. Are you new in town?"

"We are on a journey, passing through," Yiska told him cautiously.

Father Michael nodded, before repeating his original question. "Do you run?"

"There are times," Nayati answered.

"How do you feel about joining in the distance race? I've only four boys in that and they're unbeaten so far. But they need competition to sharpen themselves up if they're to win in Muirfield," Father Michael said, before adding candidly, "If you are not up to it, I'd understand."

Nayati recognised the challenge and was, as ever, unable to resist it. "How many times around the circle for this race?"

"Three and three quarters; the fifteen hundred metres," answered Father Michael.

"That is good, it will not take long," Nayati told him.

The Priest laughed and led them to the group waiting at the side of the track. "Boys meet Nayati and Yiska! They will give you four a little competition for the fifteen hundred metres," he said, pointing to the oldest.

Nayati and Yiska responded to a variety of greetings, before following Father Michael towards the start line.

The four athletes teased them a little; "We'll try not to go too fast for you," said one.

"We'll wait for you at the bend if you like," said another.

Nayati and Yiska exchanged knowing looks, accepting the underlying challenge.

Father Michael saw the exchange and their apparent confidence. 'This will be interesting!' he thought, his anticipation building.

Nayati and Yiska removed their shirts and moccasins and placed them at the side of the start line.

"Keep up with me if you can, Brother!" Nayati said to Yiska, a broad grin breaking across his face.

"I would worry for yourself, Nayati. It has been a while since we raced, and I might surprise you!" Yiska replied, returning the grin.

"You gonna run in bare feet?" asked one boy, surprised. "Aint you got no running shoes?"

Yiska answered for them both. "We don't need them," he said politely.

"Right, are you ready guys?" asked Michael. "Ready... Set... Go!"

The athletes set off fast, competing for the lead and hence the control of the race.

46

Nayati and Yiska ran comfortably behind but did not try to match the speed of the others.

"When shall we race for real?" Nayati asked Yiska as they ran.

"The last two laps," Yiska responded.

The athletes were now half a length of the straight ahead, and one turned his head and shouted something at them. Both knew that it was a tease, but they continued at their own pace.

With the finish line coming up and only two laps to go Nayati, looked at Yiska, saying, "It is time!" and they increased their pace.

With one lap to go, Nayati called out to the athletes, in front of them, "Here we come!" Once again, he and Yiska increased their pace. As they passed the others, they too increased their pace, but they were panting heavily with little left in their tanks. Nayati and Yiska were still underperforming.

"They are done, Brother! It is now you and me!" Yiska told Nayati.

"As it has been in the past and always will be," Nayati replied, increasing his pace again.

Father Michael watched the two boys speed up and leave his team well behind. "Oh, thank you sweet Lord," he called out, appreciatively at what was transpiring.

As always, Yiska and Nayati crossed the line together and Father Michael declared the race a draw, as he clapped them both on the back.

"Well done, boys!" he said to them. He turned to his four athletes and said. "I hope you learned a lesson about going off too hard at the start," he admonished them.

One of the four came up to Yiska and Nayati and shook their hands in congratulations, the other three followed his example.

Father Michael gave each of them a bottle of water, noticing that Yiska and Nayati were not even breathing hard; he knew that they had the potential to run even faster!

As the two put their shirts and moccasins back on as if to leave, Father Michael walked towards them. "Hey boys! You're not going yet, are you?" he asked.

"It is time, we must leave for there is much to do," Nayati told him.

"Well, listen a moment! We meet here daily, about three, to practice. My boys need all the help they can get; we haven't beat Muirfield once in the four years I've been running the club. If you like, you could join us. I'm sure the boys will improve their performance with you around. Why don't you come and get a burger with me and we'll talk about it!"

Yiska thought quickly, before giving an answer. Father Michael was a good person and he might have information that could help him. To Nayati's surprise, he accepted the offer. He was about to speak but Yiska gave him a stare that prevented it.

The other boys were wandering off in small groups, waving their goodbyes.

"My car's over there, and it's only a quick trip to the drive-in," Father Michael told them, leading the way.

Chapter 8:
Fast Food

Nayati looked horror-struck. "I cannot go in this," he said, looking at the old battered Ford, parked by the entrance to the track.

Yiska immediately understood the reason and turned to Father Michael, but before he responded, Father Michael spoke out, having noticed the fear on Nayati's face.

"Do you have a fear of small spaces?" he asked.

Yiska spoke for his brother. "Something like that," he said. "Perhaps we could eat together another time."

"Don't worry about the car. You see that building there?" he said, pointing down the road. "That's the drive in. Why don't we walk together? I'll come back for the car later."

Yiska nodded his agreement and Nayati's relief was obvious.

"Phobias are terrible things! They can interfere with a person's journey," said Father Michael, as they walked.

Yiska did not understand what a phobia was, but nodded anyway, glad that he didn't have to explain the real reason.

At the drive-in, Father Michael ordered burgers and fries all round with three large cokes. "After that run, I bet you both have a big appetite!" he said with a smile.

They sat at one of the picnic tables set to the side of the car park.

Nayati looked at the offerings. "This food is strange!" he stated.

"Only the nation's favourite!" Father Michael said in surprise.

Nayati put several of the fries in his mouth at once and chewed.

"It is good!" he exclaimed.

Father Michael watched him with interest. Yiska explained that there were no drive-ins where they came from and immediately regretted it as Father Michael asked that as his next question. He took a mouthful of burger and raised his eyebrows appreciatively.

Nayati liked it too. "What meat is this?" he asked.

"One hundred percent beef!" replied Father Michael, his curiosity building and a multitude of questions forming inside his mind. He tried again. "Where are you boys staying tonight?"

"We'll camp; cheaper than renting a room," Yiska told him.

Father Michael nodded, "There is another practice tomorrow afternoon. Will you come?" he asked. Yiska replied for them both, while Nayati dismantled his burger, examining the ingredients with interest.

"We're not sure; we have business to attend to in town, before we leave."

"Is there anything I can help you with?" asked Father Michael.

"Possibly," Yiska answered cautiously. "I will discuss this with my brother later."

"Boys, I'm a priest! Whatever you discuss with me, stays with me. I would not betray a confidence. If you're in any trouble, I can help."

Yiska interrupted him. "We're not in trouble; we are on a journey."

Nayati realised that the questions he'd asked about the food had raised Father Michael's interest and he responded with questions requiring more information than he and Yiska wanted to give. He changed tack and asked Father Michael to tell him about the athletics club.

"Not much to say," Father Michael started. "Four years ago, there was nothing here for the kids to do; they'd hang around in gangs, getting moved on by the Sheriff's department repeatedly. Race sorted them; there were white gangs, Indian gangs and mixed blood gangs. Clashes between them started to escalate, so I started the athletics club to bring the kids together instead. It was difficult at first, but as the club began to succeed fewer kids seemed to get mixed up in trouble. I also run a club for them in the evenings, in the hall next to the church. There are some indoor sports and games for the kids to play, or they just sit and talk over a soda. I have a colleague in Muirfield who started the same thing and with the same results."

"This is a good thing that you do," Nayati told him, impressed with the sincerity and obligation that Father Michael displayed.

"In God's eyes we're all brothers and sisters, despite our differences and the colours of our skin," Father Michael added.

Nayati spoke again. "It is as you say. Yiska is my brother by choice; we are not of the same parents."

Father Michael nodded. "Why don't you come to the club tonight? There's no charge!" Father Michael suggested. "There'll be others about your age, girls too. Some of them bake cookies or cakes on the old stove there. I think you'd enjoy it."

"It would be good to meet others of my age," said Nayati. "I will come when darkness falls."

"That's great!" exclaimed Father Michael. "Now drink your coke!"

Pushing a straw through the hole in the bottle's top, Yiska placed his mouth over the end and sucked. Nayati watched the dark liquid travel up into his mouth, then tried it too. He took a mouthful and his eyes suddenly widened in shock as the coke fizzed in his mouth. He swallowed, choking.

"It bubbles in the mouth, what trick is this?" he asked, between coughs.

Yiska laughed and even Father Michael smiled, though he wondered how this boy had never tried coke before.

Nayati laughed as well and drew in another mouthful, holding it in his mouth until it stopped fizzing.

"I like this drink," he said solemnly, and finished it without further comment.

After thanking Father Michael for the food, the two boys left, returning the way they had come. Father Michael watched them until he lost them in the heat haze of the afternoon. He'd warmed to both of them, his instinct telling him that they were decent boys. But his natural curiosity demanded answers for the questions that continued to form. They had a story to tell; he knew. How could anybody have lived to Nayati's age and never experienced burgers, fries and cokes? He smiled in amusement at Nayati's response to them and hoped that he would see them later that evening.

Yiska and Nayati walked towards their campsite.

"You liked Father Michael," Yiska stated.

"He is a man who honours his words," replied Nayati.

"I think so too. He offered privacy. As a Priest everything is confidential to him. It's the way they act and everything he does is for others," Yiska responded.

"There is risk in saying too much; it is my belief he will help us. To visit him is right, for there may be others who can help," Nayati added.

"I agree," Yiska told him.

They reached their campsite and checked their hidden things.

"We have a few hours before dark," said Yiska. "We should discuss what we want to learn before we go. If we ask too many questions, we get questions back. I noticed this earlier with Father Michael. I sensed he wanted to ask more than he did. We must not forget that we have different experiences from these people. We've not lived like them."

"It is true what you say, Yiska, I feel in the same way," Nayati responded.

"I think we should ask if there is an orphanage near here. Maybe at the club we should separate and talk to different groups. We would ask more people this way," Yiska suggested.

"It will be as you say," agreed Nayati. "Where do we say we are from?"

Yiska thought for a moment before answering. "Just say we're from a place far from here and we're on a journey of discovery. This is the truth. If they ask us for more details, we should ask a similar question back instead."

"It will be so, Brother."

As darkness fell, the two of them left the campsite and headed back into town.

"We do not know the place we travel to," Nayati stated.

"I do," answered Yiska, and he described a church to his brother.

As they approached the diner, they started to meet traffic on the road.

"How do they live with such noise?" asked Nayati.

"They get used to it."

Closer to town the traffic increased further. Flashing lights and crossings confused Nayati, and he followed his brother. People, on the streets in numbers surprised him too; it reminded him of the trading markets that he'd visited in the past with Niyol, but he was not enjoying this experience at all.

Yiska spotted the church ahead. Its tall spire with the cross on top, towered over the other flat-roofed buildings that extended around it. The building next to it was like an old barn. Made of wood, it seemed out of place beside the stonewalled church. The few windows it had were filthy with grime from the traffic, which dulled the light shining from within. Its green painted door, held open by stiff rusted hinges, invited all. A few young children sat outside on the bottom of four steps that led to it, playing a game involving sticks and a ball. There was a large sign above the door reading, 'St. Teresa's Church Youth Club', but neither Nayati nor Yiska could read it. They headed to the doorway, smiling at the giggling children and went inside.

The hall was one large space. To the rear, it had a small kitchen area with a long, narrow counter segregating it from the rest of the room. Two young girls stood behind it, one arranging biscuits on a plate, whilst the other opened a glass bottle containing a soft drink.

The opposite end of the room offered a comfortable seating area with a colourful variety of worn, but serviceable sofas, arranged around a melee of small tables. Crafted out of battered wooden crates with lengths of plywood screwed to them, they were as rustic as could be; old and worn cushions adorned them, offering a semblance of colour and comfort.

A games area dominated the rest of the open space. There were three pool tables, two table tennis tables and a skittles alley, all of which were in use by children of different ages. Two boys at a pool table saw them come in and nodded. Yiska recognised them from the afternoon's track race.

Father Michael sat on a battered, navy-blue sofa, reading to a group of small children. Nayati dipped his head in greeting as he looked up and saw the two of them. He said something to the children and called to an older boy who was standing by the kitchen area. The boy came over, took the book and continued where the Priest had left off, whilst Father Michael moved towards Nayati and Yiska.

"Hi guys, I'm so glad you came," Father Michael said to them with a big hospitable smile. "Welcome to St. Teresa's youth club! You've walked a fair way to get here, you must be thirsty. Here let me get you a drink."

He selected two bottles of coke from the kitchen and passed them one each. Nayati watched as Yiska unscrewed the cap and held the bottle to his lips. He followed the example and grinned as he enjoyed the same drink, he'd had earlier that day.

"Thank you," said Yiska, and Nayati nodded in agreement.

"What do you boys do for fun, do you shoot pool?"

Nayati looked at him not understanding what he meant. "I shoot nothing," he said, confusion on his face.

Father Michael saw the confusion and explained that pool was a game.

"Let me introduce you to some of the kids in your age group," he told them and led them to one of the pool tables. "This is Brad and Davey; you saw them earlier on the track."

The two held out their hands, and Nayati and Yiska shook them.

"Guys, meet Yiska and Nayati."

Before they could say anything, he led them to the counter and introduced them to the two girls standing behind. The girls shook hands with them before Father Michael led them away again before any opportunity of speaking took place.

Chapter 9:
Work

Father Michael led them to a sofa next and invited them to sit down.

"You said you were on a journey when we talked earlier. What sort of journey?"

"A journey to discover," answered Nayati, sensing Yiska's hesitation.

"Indulge me! Tell me more," he continued.

"We are searching for someone," said Yiska.

"Perhaps I can help," Father Michael offered.

"It is difficult," said Nayati, looking at Yiska and trying to determine his thoughts.

Father Michael followed his gaze. "Personal, none of my business, eh?" he said, giving Yiska a way out, realising that he may have been too direct.

"Personal is right," Yiska replied, not wanting to offend the kindly Priest "But…" he paused. "Maybe something you may help us with."

"Anything I can do, I will do," Father Michael told him with a smile.

Yiska nodded in acceptance. "Is there an orphanage around here?" he asked.

Whatever Father Michael had been expecting, that took him by surprise. "That's a strange question!" he commented.

Yiska said nothing, encouraging the Priest to continue.

"No orphanage in Mason; one over in Muirfield once though," he said.

"Once?" Yiska pursued.

"Yes, there's a very sad story behind it…"

Yiska held his eyes and waited for him to continue.

The Priest sighed, realising that Yiska could be as persistent as he had been.

"Let me tell you," he said. "The orphanage was closed down under a cloud of accusations, a year after I arrived in Mason. They arrested the proprietors and charged them with a multitude of crimes, ranging from child cruelty to soliciting gangs of thieves. An investigation highlighted racial segregation, with those of Indian origin dominated and bullied by the others.

"Forced to steal from local people and shops, if successful food and clothing was used as a reward and perhaps spared the beating, they would otherwise get. The dominant kids used to claim the stolen items for themselves, so the Indians always went without, which meant that often stealing continued within the orphanage. The owners sold on the stolen property and became wealthy from the process.

"When arrested, the owners denied everything and, for a while, the police believed them. Released without being charged, police found their bodies murdered in the desert. To date, their murder remains unsolved.

"As a result, they placed the remaining children in other orphanages across the state. No charges were bought against them, because of the terrible regime they had been living under. Further investigation revealed that many children were unaccounted for, having disappeared off the face of the earth. A terrible thing.

"Today the orphanage stands empty, in a complete state of disrepair; the negative publicity having deterred potential buyers."

Father Michael finished his account and shook his head. "I can't understand how people could have treated each other like that," he said, with feeling in his words.

"Anyone around who lived in that place?" asked Yiska.

"A few people still living in Muirfield I think. My friend Father Andrew would know; he knows a lot of kids, like I do here," Father Michael told him. "What's your interest?"

"We search for somebody who stayed there for a time," Nayati ventured cautiously.

"If this person had a name, it would make the search easier. I could ask around for you," Father Michael persisted.

"Why do you wish to help us? you don't even know us!" asked Yiska.

"First, helping others is the right thing to do. And second, because if I help you, you might help me in return. Favour for favour," he said, and smiled.

"How can we help you?"

"Well, I need a few days' help to repair this old building. I couldn't pay you anything, but I can offer you free board and lodging for as long as you stay," Father Michael offered.

Yiska considered this. "That sounds fair, but one problem. The boy we are searching for, his name is unknown."

"May not be such a great problem; Always ways to overcome that."

Yiska looked at him adopting a neutral look. "Seems we have a trade!"

Father Michael held out his hand for them to shake.

"Listen! Stay and meet some of the kids for a while. Have some fun! Then come back tomorrow morning about eight and I'll show you what needs doing," he said. "Now I must leave you, a conversation over there is beginning to get too heated!"

Looking around the clubroom, Nayati noticed some boys hitting balls with blunt spears on a large green tabletop and found this fascinating and puzzling! These were the boys they had beaten in the race earlier that day and, seeing Nayati's intrigue, they showed the two Navajo boys how to play pool. Neither of them showed any aptitude at it, so their new friends beat them easily, relishing their victory, having been being beaten on the track earlier on.

Later as they left the club and headed back to the camp, they discussed the events of the evening.

"We've made a good start, learning out about the orphanage, Nayati. Father Michael will help us with our search, but we'll need to trust him further," said Yiska.

"My thoughts tell me he is a good man, but his questions can be hard to answer. I do not wish to tell him what is not true and yet I cannot tell him all that is true."

"I understand. If he asks us things we are unwilling to answer, then it would be better to speak of something else," Yiska told him.

"If we are to stay in Mason for some days, we must hide our things better until we can return for them," Nayati suggested.

"That makes sense. Let's do that in the morning before we leave."

Next morning, Nayati and Yiska moved their belongings underneath an overhanging rock, covering them with small rocks and sand and marking the place with a broken-off tree branch. Then they made their way into town far too early, Nayati questioned the arrangements for the meeting.

59

"We are early," Yiska told him. "Father Michael said eight o'clock. The people here live by the clock. Time at home is different."

They waited for over an hour, before Father Michael made his appearance.

"Morning boys," he said smiling. "If it's ok with you, we could talk a little before I set you to work. Then I'll leave you and try to gather more willing folks to help."

Yiska nodded his agreement.

"Right then, I'll help you, but I need to know more about the person you're looking for," he told them, sitting down beside them and looking at Yiska for a response.

"We seek a boy about our age. He lived at an orphanage around here, but we are uncertain which one. Four years ago, he left the orphanage suddenly. He would have suffered, as he was of mixed spirits like us. Apart from that, there is nothing. We've only just started our journey and know only what you told us last night."

"Well, not to worry boys, that's a good start! We have his age, gender and the approximate time he left. You sure there's nothing else?"

"One more thing," said Yiska. "He was about four when he first arrived, taken by his mother."

"Good, present for nine or ten years. Records kept by the owners were poor, and untrustworthy, but we have enough to go on. I'll be honest though… information like this will take some time to get hold of, but I'm sure Father Andrew will help. He's lived in Muirfield at least twenty years," Father Michael told them.

Father Michael showed them planks on the side of the building that had rotted and were crumbling away, then showed them tools and a stack of lumber.

"Prise out the old planks and fit new ones. They're tongue and groove, so they slot together," he said, showing them how they fitted. "I estimate over a hundred planks need replacing, and after that the building needs repainting to protect the wood."

"When I return, I'll show you where you can sleep and get a shower for the next few days. It'll be hard work in this heat, but I think you'll both do a good job for me whilst we wait for the information," he told them.

Nayati spoke up. "We have traded well. The work we do will be good."

"I'll leave you to it then."

Yiska selected a large screwdriver and a hammer. He moved to the edge of a damaged section of wall and showed Nayati how to lever off a damaged plank. As he placed pressure against it. the wood split and broke. He removed two more before starting to fill the gap with new ones.

Wondering how he knew what to do, he guessed that he'd done this before during his stay at the orphanage.

Nayati followed his example and Yiska took pleasure in teaching his brother a new skill; so often in the past it was he that learned something from Nayati. The two of them fell into a rhythm that set them both hard at work.

Father Michael returned late in the afternoon, surprised to find the two of them still working away.

"You boys haven't stopped to eat?" he asked, running his hand over some of the repaired panels. "This is good work! I can't believe how hard you've worked to do all this! Sorry I've been so long, but I've been explaining what you need to Father Andrew and looking for more volunteers for the repair work. Folk are just too busy to help."

"We will finish this work for you as we agreed," said Nayati.

"I don't doubt that for a minute," said Father Michael. "Time to stop now though. You've worked long enough for one day. Come and share a drink with me, and I'll show you the shower and your room and you can get cleaned up. Then you can come to the club tonight and relax amongst friends."

Their temporary accommodation was one of several small rooms built at the back of the church. Just big enough for the two narrow beds placed in it, Father Andrew told them that on occasions the room had been used as temporary accommodation for homeless people during periods of bad weather.

After the Priest had left them Nayati commented that he would prefer to stay at their campsite and walk in each day. Yiska agreed but suggested that they leave a few things here for when they used the shower.

"What is this shower you speak of?" Nayati asked.
Yiska led to the door a short distance from their room and opened it. The space was the same size inside but seemed bigger, only a washbasin, toilet and shower cubical were in the space. Yiska tuned the tap and water flowed from the shower head and then laughed at the surprise on Nayati's face. Nayati moved his hand into the water that fell and exclaimed with pleasure.
"It is warm! How is this so?"
Yiska explained the essentials and Nayati looked forward to trying it.

Over the next few days, the boys worked hard finishing the repairs, until only the painting left to do. Not once during that time had they pressed Father Michael for news, trusting him to tell them when he could.

After they finished work on the fourth day, Father Michael came to them, waving a bundle of papers in his hands saying, "Good news guys! I have what you're looking for," he said and led them into the church.

This was the first time they had been inside, despite being next to the building they were repairing. They sat down on a pew together, Nayati looking round, curiosity etched in his expression. He could not take his eyes from the stained-glass windows and the large crucifix above the altar.

"People come here to speak to the spirits?"

Father Michael masked his surprise and explained.

"Have you no church where you come from?" he asked.

"Such a place is not needed. The spirits are everywhere. I speak to them when I will. Is this not the same for you?" Nayati asked.

"God is everywhere, and I can speak to him wherever and whenever I choose but we have a church, which is God's house, for people to get together and pray," answered Father Michael.

He was noticing real differences between the two boys; their experience and knowledge varied. But Nayati knew little about civilisation. The Priest hid his curiosity, he held up the papers in front of him.

"You need to read these," he said, offering them the bundle.

Yiska shook his head, "Neither of us can do that. When I try, the words dance about on the page, they will not remain still. And nobody has never taught my brother how to read."

Yiska's embarrassment was evident and Nayati spoke up, "You will read it for us?"

"Of course," replied Father Michael and started leafing through the papers.

Chapter 10:
Information

"There are several sheets here, most is legal jargon which won't mean much to you; it doesn't mean much to me either! So, I'll skip the unnecessary and get straight to the point.

"The orphanage was already full when the person you seek arrived, according to the records. We discovered, that throughout the last ten years, no adoption or fostering took place, so in theory at least, no-one left. They accepted six children into the orphanage during the right three year time period; two boys and four girls. By eliminating the girls, we're left with two boys. Both were American, but only one was 'of mixed spirits' as you call it. The records show that his name was David Chanter; Here's a picture of him here." He paused and passed Yiska a photocopy of old Polaroid photograph.

Yiska took it, his hands trembling, and gazed long and hard at the blurry image of a small boy. He looked at Nayati and nodded, passing him the picture.

"Is it your friend?" Father Michael asked.

Yiska still recovering from his initial shock, said nothing, so Nayati spoke for him. "It is him."

"That's good news! There's a little more," Father Michael told them.

"It would appear that the boy's mother left him at the orphanage. She was, dying of cancer with just a few weeks left to live. She didn't leave an address or other contact details but gave her name as Caroline Chanter. The form she completed says that the boy's father died a wartime hero, but there's no name for him either."

"That's everything my colleague discovered. Irregularities were everywhere though. Some forms, usually filled in by the authorities, were incomplete, and there's no birth certificate for the boy. The people who ran this establishment were unconcerned with keeping paperwork up to date.

There are no medical records or school records for the boy during that time. In fact, we found no records to show that he even existed after his initial entry. However, when the orphanage closed the children were sent to other care facilities around the state, David Chanter was not among them. The subsequent police investigation that took place, suggested that David Chanter left the orphanage somewhere between four and six years ago."

"That's it guys. That's all we could find out," Father Michael finished.

Nayati seemed to sense the difficulty Yiska was having trying to absorb all this information about his younger self.

"You have honoured our deal and offered much help.

For this we thank you. Tomorrow we will finish the painting and then we will leave."

"Does this information help?" Father Michael asked.

Yiska found his voice. "You told us a lot we didn't know, and this has shown me what we must do next. My brother is right; we will finish the painting and then we must go."

"Where will you go?" Father Michael asked.

"We will travel to Muirfield to visit the orphanage."

Father Michael nodded, recognising the determination behind the spoken words. "One more question," he said.

Yiska raised his eyebrows in anticipation.

"Who is this David Chanter?"

Yiska paused for a moment and Nayati spoke. "He is family."

"I thought so," said Father Michael. He passed over the sheets of paper. "These are yours now," he told them. "I must visit a sick parishioner now, so I'll leave you to it. Will I see you tonight, at the club?"

"Not tonight, but we'll return in the morning for the painting," Yiska told him.

He got up resolutely from the pew and walked out of the church followed a moment later by Nayati.

Father Michael watched them leave, feeling that there was far more to this story than so far discussed.

Yiska and Nayati headed out of town, back towards their camp site.

Nayati broke the silence that accompanied them. "There is worry in your mind, my Brother?" he stated, with concern.

"Not worry, Nayati, just overwhelmed I guess; so much to understand. We have answers, but there are more questions to ask. It is hard to live as one person and then find that you are someone else," Yiska told him.

"You are Yiska of the Navajo; there is little that can change that. Niyol has said what is important is the person you are now. You are Yiska of the Navajo. You are my brother!" he stated.

"While that is true, I need to recognise the child I used to be, to see the journey from baby to man," Yiska replied, worry still etched on his face.

"It would be good to visit the club tonight, for your mind needs rest," Nayati suggested.

But Yiska shook his head. "Too much to think about, and |I'll need your help in planning what to do next."

Nayati, recognising his brother's discomfort, answered "It will be as you say."

The two of them returned to the silent companionship they often shared, and continued walking.

They collected wood as they walked and Nayati lit a fire just as the sun was setting. Yiska opened his rucksack, took out the picture of the small boy and stared at it in the flickering light.

"You are sure it is you?" Nayati asked, breaking the silence.

"Absolutely! There's no mistake; the child here is the one I saw in my dream walk, sitting with the woman. I am worried though. I have only a name to track down records of my mother and not even that for my father. We do not know where my mother came from and there will be hundreds of Caroline Chanters across America," Yiska told him.

"Your mother died after leaving you at the orphanage. They would place her in the ground with stones, as in Mason?" Nayati asked.

"That's true, Nayati. Maybe Father Michael can help with that," said Yiska, eyes full of hope, and then continued.

"We'll finish painting the hall tomorrow and then head over to Muirfield to see the orphanage. If I recognise the inside, if it matches with what I saw with the spirits, then I'll know for sure that I'm David Chanter. But in truth I believe this already."

Nayati nodded in agreement, adding, "It is so that Father Michael's friend Father Andrew will help us in Muirfield. We will need help to read the words on paper."

Yiska nodded. "Perhaps Father Michael would arrange for us to meet with Father Andrew," he suggested.

The next morning at first light, the two of them headed back into town to paint early, to make sure they would finish the job that day.

They'd already been at work for several hours when Father Michael made his appearance. He was carrying two bottles of coke in his hands.

"Morning guys, I heard you started bright and early. Guess you could do with these," he said, offering them the drinks. "Take a break for a minute and sit with me."

Nayati grinned at him and took the coke with relish. He'd become fond of this drink with the strange, fizzing bubbles.

"You think of others Father Michael; we are thankful for it."

"Nonsense, you have more than repaid me with all your labours. It is I who am thankful for your efforts. What you've done here is important because if the building isn't in a good state of repair, the authorities will shut me down. No more youth club!"

The two boys put down their brushes and paint cans and sat down on an old and battered crate in the shadow of the wooden building to drink their cokes.

"So, what's next for you two?" enquired the priest.

"We will travel to Muirfield next," said Yiska, "I want to see where David lived, and try to find out more about his parents. There might be relatives living somewhere."

"Father Andrew might help you there, as there might be recorded information on that. It will take some time though," Father Michael offered.

"Time is ours to give!" said Yiska.

"Just an idea," said Father Michael.

Yiska raised his eyebrows.

"To show my appreciation for everything you've done, how about sharing a meal with me when you've finished here and got cleaned up? I'll drive you over to Muirfield to meet Father Andrew afterwards. He runs a similar operation to me, with a sport and youth club. There may be work too. The Lord knows it's hard to find good hands to help us with the maintenance work to our buildings," he finished.

Yiska answered for them both. "It would be good to share a meal with you and to meet your friend. We will walk though, as my brother does not travel well in vehicles. It is not so far, and we must return to collect our things from our campsite."

"Muirfield is twenty miles from here; are you sure about this?" persisted Father Michael.

"We will walk," Yiska told him.

"So be it then. Finish up here and I'll cook you a wonderful meal that my mother taught me. Trust me, you'll love it," he smiled.

"I'm looking forward to it already," Yiska told him.

Father Michael must have been keeping a discreet eye on their progress, for the minute they both appeared from their showers, he announced that dinner was ready. He invited them to sit down and placed a large, steaming dish of beef lasagne on the table in front of them. The smell was so appetising that, although neither Yiska nor Nayati recognised the meal, they looked forward to trying it. They watched Father Michael carefully and followed his lead in attacking the food with a knife and fork. Nayati fumbled with his and part of the sauce leapt from his plate onto the table.

"Took me ages to master the knife and fork," said Father Michael. "Would you prefer to use one of these?" he said, offering Nayati a spoon.

Nayati nodded his thanks.

"Tell me what do you think of that?" Father Michael asked indicating the food.

"It is not like the food I eat before," Nayati told him.

"Doli should know of this."

"Me too; it's very good!" Yiska commented.

"Lasagne, an Italian dish; just pasta, beef, tomato sauce, cheese and a special blend of herbs, the secret ingredient!" Father Michael told them. "And guess what? There's more!" and dished up another portion for them all, pleased with their response.

After they had finished eating, Father Michael thanked them again for all the work they had done.

"I'll miss you boys after you've gone, I've enjoyed meeting you and I hope that you'll consider me a friend. Anytime you need help, contact me; I'll do all that I can to help you."

The two of them muttered their thanks in return and, after spending a little longer talking about life in general they announced it was time to leave.

Father Michael gave them directions to Muirfield, telling them that if they took the cross-country route, they would save four miles of walking over following the road, then added that he would telephone his friend to expect them.

"These might come in handy," he said, passing over a parcel wrapped in brown paper and tied with string. Then they shook hands with him, said their goodbyes and left.

Chapter 11:
Trouble

They walked along Main Street towards a procession of shops that Nayati had particularly wanted to see. Yiska had explained that shops were the western world's equivalent to the trading markets and that here, they would only accept money for goods. Nayati stopped outside a large clothes shop and browsed at the goods in the window.

"The people here are not alive," Nayati said in surprise.

Yiska stifled a laugh. "They are mannequins, used to show off the clothing."

"Why do they not use people?"

"I guess nobody would want to stand, dressed up, in a shop window all day. It would be the most boring job."

"It is strange clothing. What is that on the neck?"

"The outfit is called a suit, and around the neck is a tie."

"Who would wear such clothing, it fits tight with little room to move free. It is of no use for tasks we do in the forest."

"It's not meant for the forest. Businessmen wear these. People that work in offices."

Nayati moved to the next window.

"What manner of clothing is this," he asked, with a frown of ignorance.

"Move away Nayati, don't stare at these or we will attract attention."

Nayati moved away but gave his brother a quizzical look.

"They are a lady's undergarments. Things that they wear under their main clothes."

"These will not stop the chill in the winter months."

"They're not for people in the mountains."

"Why should we not look at these?"

"These are underclothes for women not men."

"If this is so, why do they put them where men can see?"

"I can't answer that Brother," Yiska grinned.

Yiska took Nayati into a hardware store for a closer examination and the range of goods stocked, impressed him. He commented that he would need to visit several traders at a market to access the same amount of goods. Next they went into a food store and Nayati insisted that they buy a few bottles of coke to take back to the camp. He watched Yiska pass over a bill and receive a few coins as change before examining each of them carefully and listening to the names that Yiska called them.

"It is better to trade at the markets. There is no need for money."

"It's not so bad once you learn the value of each of the coins and bills," Yiska replied.

They left the shops behind and settled into a leisurely pace that gave them time to see what else the town offered. Yiska wondered why they hadn't explored it when they first arrived, rather than as they left, but the work they'd done had dominated their time.

As they rounded a corner to the road leading out of town, Yiska collided with a youth of a similar age as himself walking in the opposite direction. He grunted at the

72

impact, lost balance and grabbed at Nayati to prevent himself falling. The youth wasn't so fortunate and fell to the ground. Yiska helped him up and apologised for the accident.

"Get your hands off of me you stupid idiot. You did that on purpose didn't you? Damn half breeds why don't you watch where you're going?"

"I've already apologised there is no need to be rude. You didn't see me anymore than I saw you," Yiska answered, angered by the insults.

"You and your sort are always causing trouble wherever you go."

"And what is my sort?" Yiska snapped.

"Half breeds that's what."

Nayati stepped in between the youth and his brother. He had never seen Yiska respond in anger like he was doing now.

"Brother it is my thinking that this man wants to fight you. We should move away."

"He has no right to judge us; he doesn't know us."

Yiska pushed Nayati aside, confronting the boy.

"So where do your parents come from?"

"My dad is a Texan and my mother is Mexican but that ain't got nothing to do with you."

"You called me a half-breed, so what does that make you?"

A small crowd was gathering behind the youth, enjoying the confrontation. Somebody at the back shouted hit him and this goaded the youth to clench his fist and raise it at Yiska.

Nayati intervened a second time and spoke to the youth.

"Walk away while I keep my brother from you. It is a mistake to challenge him in this way; you will lose. Walk away."

Nayati had held the youth's eyes from the moment he had spoken and was still holding the stare. He sensed the resolve weakening in the boy and intensified the stare until the youth looked away.

"Damned half breeds," he said, before turning and walking back the way he had come from.

Someone in the crowd repeated what the youth had said and Nayati led his brother away before he responded. He set a brisk pace and soon they left the town of Mason behind.

Nayati halted and reached into the small bag that he was carrying. He took out a bottle of coke, unscrewed the lid and passed it to Yiska before repeating the process for himself.

"We have been brothers for many seasons Yiska. You always know what to do and what to say when things are difficult. This is strong in you. It is a surprise to me that you act different from the brother I am accustomed to. Why is this so?"

"You're right Nayati, I'm sorry I acted like an idiot. I couldn't help myself. If he had just called me a half-breed, I wouldn't have got so angry, but he called you one too. Nobody is going to disrespect a member of my family. You are all I have and none of you deserve that."

"I am with understanding of how it is you feel, but I have experience of this and will not give those people, who are small in thinking, reason to fear me further."

"Fear you! What do you mean fear you?"

"Grandfather has spoken to me of such matters. He says people fear what is different and what they do not understand. This is so of the man you knocked over."

"Fear or just anger. When did Niyol tell you about this?"

"When you came to our home Doli cared for you while you slept with the spirits. I went to the trade market with Niyol. I watched singing and dancing after dark and then challenged by some boys who did not like what I am. A Navajo man helped me by sending the boys away. I did not know, but they followed me back to the camp where Niyol slept and would cause trouble but for the wisdom of our Grandfather."

"You never told me this before Brother."

"I am not proud of what happened. I did not know what to do."

"I understand but we've grown and learnt a lot since then. You knew what to do today."

"It pleases me that you think this Yiska. It is so that we have learned from each other and also our Grandfather. We are as one together in many ways."

"You're right Nayati and we are stronger because of it. What else did Niyol say about this?"

"Grandfather taught about those who are Navajo, those who are not and those who are both. The Navajo tribe have many people and are related to the Apache. Those not Navajo are too many to count. Those like us are less. We are related and not related to the Navajo and we are related and are not related to those not Navajo. It causes confusion for us and those who are not us."

"This makes it complicated. Did Niyol say how to get rid of the confusion?"

"All men of different tribes are the same but not the same. It is so that we may be with any and live in peace, and it is so that we may not be with any and live in peace. All men must find out who to be with and live in peace."

"You and me. We are different and yet the same."

"We live as one! You have finished your drink and your mood is now calm, it is time for us to find our things."

"It will be as you say Nayati," Yiska replied in his best imitation of Niyol's voice.

Nayati laughed. "Has our grandfather heard you speak in the manner of his voice?"

"He has not."

"That is a good thing."

Yiska and Nayati made their way back to their campsite.

"We met some good people, Nayati," said Yiska as they walked.

"It is true what you say, Brother, but they follow strange ways," replied Nayati.

Yiska grinned at him. "I am sure they would find our ways strange too. Our journey has started well, we've discovered a lot, but there is still more to discover. I hope we are as lucky in Muirfield," Yiska continued.

"There is Father Michael's friend to help."

Yiska nodded. "The people who live here have different ways from those you are used to."

"There are good things, and things that are not good," Nayati replied. "I like the drink with bubbles. I like the warm water that appears from metal pipes. I like meeting with others of our age."

Yiska grinned at his first two descriptions. "What do you not like?" he asked.

"The people are always in a hurry. There is no quiet place. Some people stare at you in a ways that mean they do not like what they see," Nayati replied.

"Could you live here?"

Nayati paused before answering. "There is reason to be here with you, so I will accept new ways and learn what I can. Without reason there is nothing for me to stay. The people I care for are not here."

"I miss them too and our life in the mountain. Once I have finished my journey, I will go back; we will go back." Yiska told him.

Nayati remembered the parcel he'd been carrying and drew his knife to cut the string. Inside the wrapping paper were two sets of used but fresh clothes.

"Father Michael is a generous man," said Yiska in appreciation.

Chapter 12:
Yahzi

The next morning they broke camp and started the long trek to Muirfield. Yiska realised that, apart from being a shorter route, travelling across country and not following the road, meant that they would avoid meeting inquisitive people and would be away from the noise that offended his Brother.

Muirfield was a town very like Mason that also fringed the desert and was situated due north of it. Yiska suggested they travel all day to search and find a place to camp before nightfall. Town could wait until the following day, after leaving their belongings concealed to lighten their load as they had done in Mason.

The town loomed ahead of them as their journey drew to a close but there was no suitable place to make a camp. Further on and to the east of the town, Yiska saw a large area of uneven ground scattered with boulders and smaller rocks and pointed it out to Nayati, who nodded in instant understanding and altered his direction.

Reaching it, they found a place to make a temporary camp that would serve them for the duration of their stay. There were still a few hours of daylight left, even though the sun's colour deepened as it descended the azure sky, and Yiska wondered about heading into town. Although they had water with them, they'd not eaten since the meal with Father Michael. "We need to get some food?"

"It would be good to eat for we have travelled far," Nayati responded.

"Let's wait for darkness and find a drive-in." Yiska suggested.

"I will eat many of their burgers and drink the bubbles from the tins," Nayati said, his eyes smiling as he thought of the coke that he enjoyed so much. He brought out the money that Niyol had given him and looked at the range of notes. As yet he'd spent none, preferring to leave that to his brother, but he knew things would be different now.

Niyol had arranged the bills in order of value and had instructed both the boys to remember the value of each by recognising the colour and the portrait on each type. Yiska selected three ten-dollar bills from the wad and put them in his pocket. Nayati packed away the rest with their belongings that would remain hidden at the camp.

Just as the sun set, they left camp and started to walk the two miles towards the now illuminated town. Vehicles on the move gave them a target and they altered their direction to intersect the road that must be ahead. Father Michael had told them that most drive-ins were situated outside of town, and they were pleased to see a neon sign shining bright at the side of the road ahead. There was no mistaking the image of a burger above it. Yiska pointed it out to Nayati who grinned, expecting the promised meal.

As they approached the entrance to the diner, a female voice from the shadows called out.

"You got any spare cash, Mister, just need enough for food."

Nayati stepped towards the voice, stopping so abruptly that Yiska bumped into him.

"Why do you sit in the dark?" Nayati asked the figure sitting on the ground.

"I'm not welcome here because I haven't any money to buy food," replied the figure.

The girl was small, probably young, but it was too dark to be sure.

"If you need food, why do you not go home to get some?" Yiska suggested.

"Don't have a home, Mister," answered the voice.

"Where is it that you sleep?" Nayati asked.

"Wherever I lay down," came the response from the shadows. "Well? Can you spare me any money for food then?"

"Wait here while my brother and I buy food. We will share with you what we get," Nayati told the voice. "Come, Brother!" he commanded and led the way through the doorway.

Yiska ordered burgers, fries and cokes and offered the waitress a bill.

"That's not enough!" she told him, before accepting a second note from him.

Yiska and Nayati picked up the bags of food and headed for the door but halted when the waitress called them back. "You forgot your change!" she said and gave Yiska a few coins.

Outside they found an empty table and set the food down. Nayati headed to where the voice had come from.

"We have food, come and share it with us," he invited.

"No, leave it here!" the voice commanded.

Nayati was annoyed at the response.

"It is the custom that when a person shares food with another, they eat at the same table," he said. "The food is at my table. If you wish to eat, join us!" He turned, going back to the table.

Yiska looked at him and raised his eyebrows, but Nayati said nothing and instead reached for a burger and took a large mouthful. "This is good!" he said, voice raised and projected towards the shadows.

"Yes, very good," agreed Yiska.

Nayati finished an entire burger before a small noise caught his attention and the person from the shadows appeared by the table. He pointed to the empty seat opposite him and a burger, still wrapped in paper, on the wooden table in front of it. The person sat and immediately grabbed the food, with grubby hands. Nayati pushed some fries and a coke towards his guest, making eye contact for the first time.

He looked at a girl a little younger than himself. Her eyes were dark brown and her skin dark; there was no mistaking she was an Indian.

"By what name are you known?"

"I am called Yahzi," she told him, unable to take her eyes off of his.

"I am Nayati and this is my brother, Yiska."

She nodded, still unable to break eye contact. "They are Navajo names like mine," she said. "Nayati means 'He who wrestles' and Yiska means the night has passed."

"It is as you say," Nayati agreed, "But I have not known a Navajo called Yahzi."

"It means 'Little one'," she told him. "I didn't grow much as a baby and I haven't since!" She smiled for the first time, as if she had found what she said amusing.

Nayati noticed the perfect white teeth between gentle lips and warmed to her.

The questions stopped for a while as Nayati and Yiska started on a second burger. Yiska pushed the last one towards Yahzi.

"Go ahead! It is clear you've not eaten," he encouraged.

She did not hesitate devouring it as quick as the first, before looking around and standing up.

Her name is accurate, thought Yiska as her full height fell short of five foot.

"I thank you for the food," she said, and moved away into the shadows.

Nayati called out "Wait!" but she had gone.

"You meet different people on a journey, that's for sure," said Yiska.

"I believe her life is difficult, for she has no home, no food and looks dirty. This is not right," Nayati said.

Yiska recognised an unusual look on his brother's face but wasn't sure what it meant.

"You are right, Brother; I think she is a street person. You did a good thing offering her food," Yiska told him. "Let's start back; I need a good night's sleep."

They head back towards their camp.

The next morning they walked back into town. Yiska sought Father Andrew first, Finding the church should be easy but was more difficult than he had expected and Yiska stopped an elderly lady to get directions. Unlike in Mason, where the church was in the middle of town, this one was at the furthest end. It was, in fact, the last building before the road led off towards another town thirty miles away.

As they approached it, they saw that the church was older than Mason's, and that, although built of stone, one side showed repairs, made in the past with wood rather than the original materials.

Yiska opened the door and called out a greeting. While he waited for a response, he noticed the simple layout of the inside. Two rows of pews bisected a central aisle that led to the raised altar at the far end of the church. Kneeling cushions, arranged in a row in front of it, were behind a low rail. All the windows were stained glass, except the main one behind the altar, through which white light flowed.

A figure dressed like Father Michael appeared from a small door next to the altar.

"Hello yourself!" smiled a portly man in his early fifties, making his way towards them. "You have to be Yiska and Nayati! Father Michael said you might drop by. I've been hearing complimentary things about you two. Glad to meet you, boys! Father Andrew," he said, offering his hand.

Yiska shook it, introducing himself and his brother, and looked at the Priest's ruddy complexion and green eyes. He returned the smile thanking Father Andrew for the help he had given Father Michael.

"You boys did a good thing in repairing the youth club down in Mason; the authorities had been planning to close it down. Father Michael said he would be forever grateful to you! Look, we can't stand here in the doorway! Come on in and join me in a cup of coffee, and tell me how I can help you," he said, ushering them towards the door he had emerged from.

Chapter 13:
Orphanage

The Priest used the space as a changing room. On a sideboard, an electric kettle and a few cups awaited. He motioned for them to sit at a table that was only big enough for two.

"Do you take sugar and milk, or do you prefer it straight?" Father Andrew asked.

Yiska remembered how Niyol made his and replied, "Just coffee, please."

Father Andrew brought the cups over and squeezed in beside them.

"Father Michael said you were walking over from Mason; few walk that sort of distance these days," he said.

"How can I help you boys?"

Yiska told him that he would like to see the orphanage where David grew up.

"Hmm! I should be able to arrange that. The place has been empty since they closed it down. It's up for sale, but there's been little interest, it's rather run down and the cost of repair would be hefty. I have a friend who works in real estate in town who might lend me the key. When do you want to go?" he asked.

"As soon as possible please," responded Yiska.

"No time like the present then! Why don't we finish our coffee and walk into town and see what we can arrange?" Father Andrew suggested.

"We'd like to repay you for the all the help you've given us," Yiska told him.

"The church always needs help and I appreciate your offer. There is something you can help with, but the hours are rather unsociable," Father Andrew responded.

"The hours are not a concern. What's the work?" asked Yiska.

"We'll discuss it later. Right now it's time to go!"

Yiska rose from his seat and followed Father Andrew outside, with Nayati close behind.

"Nothing more I like doing than solving mysteries and investigating things," Father Andrew said, setting a brisk pace back towards town.

When they reached the real estate offices, he asked the two of them to wait while he entered. He returned quickly, brandishing a key in front of him.

"That was easy!" he said. "Follow me!"

Once more he set off at a rapid pace, and headed east down a long, wide street with a variety of stores and offices. After a few minutes' walk, the buildings ceased, and the street narrowed, and started to head out of town.

Following its direction with his eyes, Yiska made out a large building less than half a mile away. He knew instinctively that this was it. As they approached, he hoped something would trigger a memory inside his head; but nothing came. They diverted from the road onto a dirt track winding its way toward the front entrance, and then they were there, standing in front of two massive oak doors.

"There were over sixty children housed here at its peak," Father Andrew told them as he placed the key in the lock and turned it. A small clicking noise followed by an eerie creak, broke the silence as he pushed the door open.

They stepped into a large hallway, wide enough to drive a station wagon through.

Father Andrew turned to Yiska. "It hasn't been altered since it was occupied."

"The children's rooms?" Yiska asked.

"I've been here several times, all the rooms are identical," he said.

The Priest led the way down a long corridor, leaving footprints on the shabby, dust-covered linoleum. He stopped outside the first door; slid back the two iron bolts holding it closed and pushed open the door.

Inside the room were eight iron-framed beds; four along each side, positioned beneath a pair of narrow, barred windows. The mattresses were missing. Beds were separated by wooden cupboards. Each had three drawers to the left and a space for hanging clothes to the right. Yiska knew this was the place. He turned, and left the building, stopping by a large oak tree and sitting down in its shade.

Nayati and Father Andrew followed him outside, with the latter locking the front door. They moved towards Yiska and sat down alongside; neither speaking until Yiska broke the silence.

"How could they allow just two people to look after so many children?"

"That's just it, they didn't. Everybody round here believed they were good people, but they were good at hiding the truth. The kids looked after themselves; they cleaned, they did most of the cooking, they did everything! At night, the owner took them places to break in and steal. The suffering they endured here must have been awful, and worse, probably still continues for those whose memories won't let them forget," he said, and it was clear he felt the sadness.

"The bolts on the doors, and the bars on the windows, showed they were like prisoners, locked in. How did they explain that?" Yiska asked.

"They were for the children's own protection; to prevent newcomers from running away. Sometimes they were open because locals saw them playing in the yard. All appeared to be normal from anybody that passed by. It just wasn't like that on the inside," Father Andrew told them.

"Father Michael told us that several children went missing over the years. Do you know how many?" Yiska pursued.

"Well, the records are incomplete but at the time of closure, the police believe that there were seventeen children unaccounted for; seventeen that disappeared from the place during its last ten years," Father Andrew continued, shaking his head in disbelief. "God alone knows what happened to the poor wretches," he finished.

Father Andrew looked at Yiska who had suddenly slumped to one side.

"What's wrong with your brother?" he asked Nayati, concern in his voice.

Nayati moved in and gently laid his brother onto his back. "My brother is no longer with us. He walks with the spirits," he said in a solemn tone.

"What do you mean?" asked Father Andrew, reaching across to check for the pulse in Yiska's neck.

"Do not concern yourself, this has happened before. He will sleep and all will be well again," Nayati replied gently.

"Is he sick? Does he need some medication or something?" he asked, sounding worried now.

"He needs nothing. I will stay with him until he wakes. If you need, you can go. I will bring him to you later, so that you can see all is well," Nayati said patiently.

"Go! I cannot leave somebody in this condition," Father Michael said, horrified at the suggestion.

"Then you must stay with me until he wakes," Nayati told him. "He is safe, for his animal spirit watches over him," he added, pointing to the eagle circling silently above their heads.

Father Michael remained silent for a while, his mind in turmoil as he contemplated what to do. On the one hand, he had what appeared to be a sick boy lying unconscious beside him, who may need medical attention, whilst on the other he had Nayati who remained calm and sat like a guard next to his brother, unconcerned by Yiska's predicament.

"Tell me more, young man, or I'm going into town to get help!"

Nayati sensed Father Andrew's fear and concern. "I will tell you enough to still your concerns, Father Andrew, but understand this. What I tell you is not for others," Nayati said, in a determined voice. "You will agree to this?"

"I am a Priest! Whatever you entrust to me, stays with me," Father Andrew replied.

"That is what Father Michael said, and I learned to trust him. I will trust you also."

"Yiska is my brother but we do not share the same parents. There was a time when my grandfather discovered Yiska in the desert, almost dead. Someone had beaten and left him to die. My grandfather cared for him and brought him home until he was well. When he woke, he had no memories of who he was. He knew nothing of himself or life before waking. He has visited the spirits many times, as he does now. When he wakes, the spirits will have returned memories to him," Nayati told him.

"I understand," Father Andrew whispered "But tell me, how is he when he wakes up? And how long does he sleep for?"

"When he wakes, there is pain, for a short time. He sleeps for different times. Many hours at first, but each time it is less," Nayati explained.

"How long the last time?" Father Andrew asked.

"How long is dawn until noon?" Nayati answered with a question.

Father Andrew nodded. "I'll go to the church and get my car, then we could take him somewhere more appropriate," he suggested.

But Nayati shook his head. "Grandfather says for us not to move him when this happens. He is wise and knows about these things. I will stay here with him until he wakes."

"I'll stay as well and we will watch over him together," said Father Andrew.

An hour passed without further conversation, until Father Andrew broke the silence. "How long has Yiska been with you Nayati?" he asked.

"Five years when the summer ends," Nayati told him.

"I think I understand," Father Andrew told him, as his brain processed the information he'd learned.

"What is there to understand?" Nayati asked.

"Your Brother and David Chanter; they are the same? David Chanter became Yiska when he lost his memory. You want to find out who Yiska was," Father Andrew said.

Nayati looked at him, unable to hide his surprise. "It is as you say!" he said, nodding his head in affirmation. "No other who knows this."

"That will remain the same Nayati," said Father Andrew. "I worry for your brother for different reasons," he said. "The things he'll learn will not be easy to live with. There will be shame at what he was forced to do to survive."

"He is different now, he knows what is important; he is Yiska of the Navajo," said Nayati with total confidence."

"That may be so. But a good person experiences guilt for the things he's done wrong and this can change the way they think about themselves," Father Andrew said.

"You are wise, as my grandfather! We travel this journey together. I will look for changes in my brother. I will help him as he would help me," Nayati stated with a degree of certainty.

"He is lucky to have a brother like you," Father Andrew said.

"I am lucky also. Yiska saved my life once, and the life of my sister."

Father Andrew looked down at Yiska, just in time to see him roll his head to one side and moan.

"My brother wakes!" said Nayati.

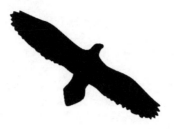

Chapter 14:
Past Sins

The boy lay on the old iron framed bed as darkness fell, waiting for the call. He had been through the routine a dozen times before; the waiting was always the worst part. He contemplated what they would force him to do. They would come for him soon. If it was early, then they would travel a greater distance. He didn't wait long. The scraping rasp of the bolts being drawn back alerted him. Iron bolts that kept him there; a prisoner condemned to a life he had not chosen.

The door creaked open and two large figures armed with baseball bats emerged at his bedside. One of them prodded him in the stomach with the bat.

"It's time," a voice whispered, "let's go!"

He rose from the bed, falling in behind one of the shadowy figures; the other followed behind, his bat pushed into the boy's back. They stopped to open a bolted door, then headed down the hallway towards the front entrance. The huge oak door was already open and framed a large, well-built man dressed in black who waited silently. He led them out to the old black van; a van that also became a prison once inside.

The rear doors were open, revealing the bench seats positioned along both the sides and behind the cab. They were all dressed in black. Two, judging by their size, were almost adults; the third, a small child. The boy and his two guards climbed in the van and the well-built man closed the door behind them and entered through the driver's door.

"It's a long drive people, so get some rest if you can," he laughed, knowing they would not rest at all on their uncomfortable seats, and the worry of what they would do when they arrived.

The engine started, and the van moved away. He pictured the route as it meandered down the orphanage driveway and turned onto the main road and could only wonder what unknown destination it headed toward. They travelled the journey in total silence, expected practise, demanded of all of them, until the van parked and stopped. The driver stepped out and walked round to the rear of the van, opening the door.

"Out," he whispered, "and don't make a sound!"

They stood in a circle awaiting instructions; the boy and the smaller child surrounded by the others. The driver grabbed both of them by their clothing just below the neck and pressed his face close against them.

"Do what you're told," his whispered voice spat at them.

Neither said anything; already experienced at these visits, they'd learnt quickly.

The man passed round black balaclavas and gloves to the larger members of the gang and gave a tin of boot polish to the boy.

"Do it now!"

He opened it and put his fingers into the slippery polish. Rubbed in on face and hands, he blended into the darkness before turning and repeating the process on the smaller child, hiding his surprise when he realised that this one was a girl.

Isolated and quiet, he wasn't privy to the location. The darkness was intense, with the new moon yet to reveal itself. As his eyes grew accustomed to it, the boy could only just make out the winding track they followed. They rounded a bend, and an enormous house stood, illuminated by soft lights set at ground level and directed upwards. The effect made the house appear even larger and gave it an ethereal quality that sent a chill down the boy's spine. The surface under his feet changed and become softer as they cut across manicured lawns.

They edged their way around to the rear entrance. One of the group shoved the girl forward.

"Do it! Through the dog flap and open the door," the leader said, forcing the girl down.

The boy watched as she started to wriggle through, first her head, then her torso, until she got stuck, her hips just too wide to get through the narrow space. Try though she did, she could go no further.

The leader lost his patience and yanked her out; ignorant of the fact that she'd smashed her head against the side of the flap. She made no sound though, even as blood from a gash trickled slowly down her face.

"Looks like Plan B then!" The leader announced.

At that, the four larger members of the group split into pairs and disappeared in opposite directions, leaving the two smaller ones with the leader.

"Sit!" he hissed and the two of them obeyed without hesitation.

An owl hooted, high above their heads, and forced a shiver to run down the boy's spine. After a few minutes the others returned. One pointed back the way he'd appeared from and they all followed him around to the side of the building, stopping at a window positioned at adult head height. It had a small opener at the top wedged open, because of a broken retainer.

The boy moved forward expecting what was coming next. The leader lifted him up whilst another opened out the window to its fullest extent. Then feet first, the leader inserted him through the window. He kept his legs stretched out until his hips passed through and then slowly lowered them searching for purchase on a piece of furniture or windowsill. It was a utility space and his feet touched down onto a washing machine.

The leader held his grip and thrust his masked face into the boy's.

"You've got two minutes."

The menacing threat in his eyes goaded the boy on. He released his grip, and his torso, then head, slipped through, and he disappeared from sight. The gang made their way back to the rear entrance and waited.

It was less than a minute before the boy had found his way to the door, unfastened the lock and opened it. The leader sent in the four older members of the group whilst he remained outside with the two youngest, who he sat tight against the wall.

The boy wiped away some of the blood from the girl's head with his sleeve and placed a protective arm around her.

Fifteen minutes later, the older boys returned carrying lightweight cloth sacks bulging with goods they had stolen from the house. They returned the same way back to the van and loaded their goods between their seats.

The driver started the engine and pulled away.

"Another successful day at the office boys!" he called out. "You'll eat well tomorrow."

The younger boy dropped his head assuming responsibility for them gaining access and the subsequent burglary. He was fully aware it was wrong, and unlike the older male members, his conscience nagged at him. The girl lay her head against his shoulder and closed her eyes trying to ignore the pain that throbbed from her wound. He put his arm around her for the second time.

As the images faded and disappeared, Yiska heard his Brother's voice gently calling to him. He opened his eyes and winced at the pain that hit him like a bolt of lightning. He moaned. His vision gradually cleared, and his eyes focused upon the orphanage once more.

"You walk with the spirits?" Nayati asked him.

"Yes," Yiska replied, trying to sit up.

"Are you all right, boy?" Yiska heard another voice ask. He turned his head to see an anxious-looking Father Andrew.

"Imagine being hit with a club, that describes it pretty well, but it will soon pass," Yiska responded. "How long was I out for?" he asked.

"About four hours, I'd say," answered Father Andrew.

"You've been here the whole time?" asked Yiska.

"He has been here, Brother," Nayati answered.

"I'm sorry I caused you all this wasted time, Father Andrew," Yiska said.

"Nonsense, boy! I am blessed to do God's work, and to his credit, the challenges and tasks he sets me are always thought-provoking and interesting," he replied. "If you can walk, we should start back. You need to drink and rest, I suspect."

A short while later, Yiska was ready to attempt the journey back to the church. They took their time and Father Andrew insisted that they stop at a diner for a drink on the way.

Afterwards, he stopped at a small dwelling, a hundred yards away from the church. "Welcome to my home, boys! It's not much, but it serves the purpose."

They entered a hallway that led into a sitting room.

Father Andrew offered Yiska the couch and told him to put his feet up. Yiska declined the second part; he was tired, but otherwise back to himself. The Priest brought them coffee and sat down opposite.

"Whilst you were 'out', Yiska, your Brother and I had a good conversation. You are David Chanter and once lived at the orphanage. He didn't betray you; I worked it out for myself. What I've learned Yiska, will remain with me alone unless you give me permission to divulge it."

"They forced the children to do terrible things there, things that can affect them to their detriment. If you wish to discuss those things; I, as God's servant, am here for you. Although, I doubt any of the residents of that orphanage would want to relive their experiences."

"You're correct, Father Andrew and considerate. The memories I've just received are unpleasant and I'm not yet ready to discuss them, but I thank you for your offer," Yiska replied.

"Father Michael told me that you needed my help, but surely it wasn't just to visit the orphanage. So tell me, what is it that I can help you with?" Father Andrew asked.

Yiska nodded. "What I want, is information about my real parents. There has to be more?" Yiska asked.

"There will be more to discover Yiska. We have your mother's name and her approximate year of death; there should be records somewhere. Your father may be more of a challenge, though we should be able to find his name at least from a marriage certificate. I'll put things in motion, but it will be time-consuming. I doubt we will find much locally and most of the information we seek will be further afield."

Nayati spoke next. "There is a way for us to help you also?"

Father Andrew smiled. "Yes, there is. I run a small mobile soup kitchen in town. I need some volunteers to work from it," he told them. As both boys looked confused, he explained what he meant. "It's a mobile food van for people who have no jobs, money, or a home; street people. The van sets up in a quiet part of town and remains open from ten until two in the morning. I've been so busy with the athletics club and youth club on top of my church commitments, that I've been wearing myself rather thin with this. I just can't seem to find enough volunteers to help."

"Do we have to cook the food?" Yiska asked.

"Oh no, no, no!" laughed Father Andrew, "the food is mostly leftovers from two of the restaurants in town. Two lovely ladies collect it each day and turn it into soup or broth. The soup then goes to the van ready to share out. Simple, but it has become so important for the homeless."

"We will help you as you ask and begin tonight."

"Thank you, thank you both! This means a lot to me. I don't want to close the kitchen down, and it's been looking like that might be my only option. I just wish there were others who would come forward and offer their help," Father Andrew told them. "You'll need accommodation for at least a month. I've a friend in town that can put you up for a small price. She won't provide food, but she won't mind you coming home late from the soup kitchen if you're quiet. What do you say? A bed each and a shower when you need it?"

"More convenient than camping for this length of time. How much would it cost?" Yiska asked.

"It will be cheap because you are working for the church. She has helped like this before. Do you have money?"

Yiska nodded.

"Good, I'll arrange it and take you over before you start work tonight. Let's meet here at eight o'clock. You'll have to excuse me for now boys, there's a lot to do, but feel free to stay and rest for as long as you need!"

Chapter 15:
Disclosure

The brothers left Father Andrew's house and walked back towards their campsite. Although accustomed to long periods of comfortable silence between them, Nayati sensed his brother's discomfort. Yiska walked, oblivious to anything around him and having twice collided with people walking towards him.

"I wish to visit the diner. I need the drink with bubbles."

The words stimulated Yiska to break the thoughts that were dominating his mind.

He laughed. "You seem to need this drink often Brother. Can it be true that you have found something from western society that you like?"

"It is as you say. I was wrong with my thinking."

"Could it be that you want to stay for longer than the purpose of our journey?"

"I will not stay longer than our purpose. It is so that I am without my home, my family."

"It's not as bad as you imagined it would be?"

"Grandfather's words told to me to learn about the ways of the western people. I must watch and listen; I must not judge the people different from us. It is as he says."

"The people do not speak as we do. Some are very direct and others who talk around things rather than discuss. It's difficult, and I suppose that I am one of them."

"You are one of them in times of the past. Now you are one with those you live with."

Yiska let conversation cease as they approached the diner not wanting to dwell on the subject that reminded him of how much he too missed their family and Doli.

He drew a bill from his pocket and passed it to Nayati.

"It's time that you practised buying something. Order the drinks, pay for it and wait for the change."

Nayati nodded. "It will be as you say, and I will get more for when we reach our camp."

"Since you can't seem to go for long without a coke, that's a good idea."

"You will wait at the tables outside. I will order food so there will be no need of food at our camp."

Yiska took a seat at a table while his brother entered the diner. He watched through the window as two of the waitresses almost fought to serve the handsome young man. Yiska smiled at their antics, fully used to the effect on females Nayati's appearance had and smiled at the serious look on his brother's face as he went about his purchase. He made a mental note to explain the difference between buying with money and trading goods for good.

Nayati returned with food and drinks and pushed them forward.

"It is my thought that since Niyol is not here that you would talk about your dream walk with your brother. I will consider what you tell me, as our grandfather would, and give my thoughts on this."

Yiska was about to suggest that he would talk about it later when he realised the responsibility Nayati was undertaking on his behalf. To discuss and interpret the spirits and the spirit world was a delicate matter to the untrained and as far as he was aware Niyol had not educated Nayati about this. But his brother was prepared to take the responsibility for him.

"The spirits showed me more this time Nayati."

"It is so that when you walk with the spirits, the memories are not good."

"You're right there! The only good thing that I can remember from any of these dreams was seeing my mother. It was painful but seeing her was amazing, precious even."

Between mouthfuls of fries and coke Yiska related the details of the latest memories released to him. Nayati listened carefully and even after his brother had finished, he remained quiet.

"Well?" Yiska asked, breaking the silence.

"I would consider this for a while, as Niyol would, the meanings seem clear. I will think as we walk to camp."

An hour later they were back in the quiet of their campsite. Nayati had adopted a serious look on his face and had not spoken since they had left the diner. Yiska didn't press him to hurry in his deliberations, it just wasn't their way. Things took as long as they took. He already had his own views on what the spirits revealed. Nayati had been right. It didn't seem all that complicated.

They sat side by side watching the sun dip below the horizon before Nayati spoke again.

"You are ready to hear my words. You are the boy. They keep you like a rabbit in a snare. You are not there from choice. Sinew holds the rabbit; iron bolts hold you. The places you visit are unknown to you. You open doors for them, and they take what does not belong to them. It is unknown why they do this, but it is wrong. This is your life in this place. Perhaps they give you things for doing this."

Nayati fell silent and Yiska responded.

"The reason they stole the belongings of others is so that they can sell them for money. People mostly steal for money, though not all. You're right about this life for the children of the orphanage. All of us started as the girl in the memories. As we got older, they used us for different things. The reward was food. I was a thief, a bad person."

"You have no choice in what you did."

"There is always a choice Nayati, and I made the wrong one."

"The brother of mine is not a bad person."

"Not now, but once..."

"Even in the bad there is good."

"How so?"

"The girl, you wiped away her blood and comfort her with your arm. You comfort her again in the van. A bad person would not do this."

"I wasn't strong enough not to do what was wrong though"

"You could not go against the will of the elders."

"I know but it doesn't change the way I feel about it."

"The spirits show you how you live before Grandfather found you in the desert. The spirits told you nothing of your life at the orphanage before now. They do this to spare you of the pain. You could not live in peace at the cave with such knowledge. We will find the truth with Father Andrew and the spirits know that you are strong to show you this."

"Thank you for what you said Nayati. Niyol would agree with your interpretation of the dream walk, and he would be proud of the fact that you becoming as wise as he."

Nayati nodded his acceptance of what Yiska had said but held back his continuing concern about how Yiska viewed his past. His grandfather, and even his sister, would say the person he was becoming was more important. Despite this, Yiska wanted to focus on the bad rather than the good.

He remembered Father Andrew's words about how those who had lived through this, might find it difficult and he made a mental note to talk to the Priest about this when he got the chance.

With the light almost gone they selected some of their belongings to take into town, concealing everything they left behind under a pile of small rocks.

"It will be that we sleep in a strange place tonight," Nayati stated.

"I'm guessing that it will be a good place, after all it belongs to a friend of Father Andrew."

"It will be good to have the hot water from the metal pipes on my body again," Nayati said.

Yiska grinned. "The shower is good. And we will wash our clothes. If we are dirty, we will be branded as street people."

"The work we do for Father Andrew. Night is a strange time to feed people of the streets."

"It makes sense when you understand that the food comes from restaurants. They wouldn't be enough leftovers earlier in the day. Once collected, it's turned into a soup or a broth. Doing it late at night also gives the street people some privacy. Non street people don't like seeing them during the daytime. There is less likely to be trouble."

"To people they are different, as those who are of mixed spirits?"

"Yes."

"We should teach them of the thinking's of our grandfather."

"That we can learn from those who are different?"

"It is a better way."

"If only things were that easy."

Chapter 16:
Paying Their Way

Half an hour later they made their way into town. Finding their way to Father Andrew's house was not as straightforward as they expected. None of the streets they travelled along looked the same as they had during the daylight hours. Eventually, they found it just as Father Andrew stepped out.

"Bang on time boys" he greeted them cheerfully, "Follow me!"

They walked the length of the street before veering left to a row of houses were small and single storey. Father Andrew opened a small gate in a white picket fence and followed the path to the front door. The door opened before he could knock, and a pleasant-looking, middle-aged woman appeared before them.

"Hello, Mrs Willoughby!" said Father Andrew brightly. "These are the friends I mentioned. This is Yiska, and this is Nayati."

She looked them up and down saying with a stern expression and then with an equally stern voice, "You'd better come in."

Ushering them all into the small living space, she invited them to sit down, presenting each of them with a cup of tea.

Yiska noticed she hadn't asked them how they liked the drink; she was set in her ways. She watched the boys carefully as they sipped politely at the scalding tea.

Nayati spoke first. "What is it that you call this drink?"

"Why, it's tea!" she said defensively. "Have you never had tea before?" she asked quickly.

"I have not," replied Nayati. "It is good!"

The woman gave Father Andrew an inquisitive glance, before saying that she was glad he liked it.

"My sister makes tea from herbs and flowers and the bark of the willow tree."

"I would love to learn about that." The woman said smiling.

Mrs Willoughby took the next half an hour up by informing them of all the house rules of which, Nayati thought, there were many.

Yiska however listened carefully, pleased that they were free to come and go whenever, as long as they were quiet, so he paid a month's rent in advance, much to Mrs Willoughby's surprise. They followed her down the hallway to their room, which contained two single beds, a closet and a chest of drawers. Although small, with little space between the furniture, it was spotless, and looked comfortable and cheerful with its autumn leaf pattern on the matching curtains and bedspreads.

Yiska nodded his satisfaction and placed down his bag on top of the chest of drawers. He removed the clothes and was about to put them into a drawer when Mrs Willoughby stopped him.

"This is all you have?"

Yiska nodded, explaining that they were travelling light.

"Well, they need washing; I'll make a trade with you. I need some wood chopped for the fire tomorrow. You do that and I'll wash your clothes. Do we have a deal?"

Yiska beamed his best smile at her, which took her by surprise and compelled her to reciprocate.

"A good deal," he answered.

Father Andrew noticed the exchange and was pleased. She would love these two and treat them like her own, and he suspected that the boys would warm to her.

"Well, sorry to interrupt, Mrs Willoughby, but it's time I introduced these two to the soup kitchen," he told her. "God's work calls!"

"Of course!" she replied and led them back into the narrow hallway. "Bathroom's in here," she said pointing to another door. "There'll be fresh towels on your beds when you come back."

She held up two keys and gave one each to the boys,

"You'll need these to get back in when you've finished. I'll see you tomorrow, goodnight."

As they left the house, Father Andrew told them what a fine woman Mrs Willoughby was.

"If necessary, we can trust her with a confidence. Maybe we might enlist her research skills over the coming weeks," he told them.

Two streets away and parked at the end of a vacant lot stood the soup kitchen. There were already people standing around the vehicle, as the kitchen's patrons awaited its opening.

Father Andrew unlocked the rear door and entered. Inside was a small counter with a huge pan of thick soup collected earlier, some large paper bags of crusty bread rolls, a stack of bowls and a pile of spoons. A small gas powered stove stood to the side of the counter and Father Andrew showed Yiska how to turn on the propane gas and light it. He moved the pan onto the flame and stirred it with a large wooden spoon from underneath the counter. After filling a large kettle with water from a container, he set it on the stove to heat. He retrieved a huge catering tin of coffee from under the counter, a tin of sugar and some mugs and teaspoons from a cupboard on the wall. He handed a spoon to Yiska and told him to make up a large pot of coffee. Within ten minutes the water boiled for the coffee and the soup was bubbling merrily away with gentle plopping sounds. Father Andrew instructed Yiska to serve the coffee and Nayati to ladle the soup into bowls and hand it out with the bread.

"I think we're about ready to open," he told them happily, and motioned Nayati to follow him outside.

Father Andrew unlocked two padlocks at the side of the van holding down a flap which formed an awning when raised, providing shelter at the counter. He raised the flap and locked it in place with metal poles inserted into retainer slots at the bottom of the van. With this done he slid open the two windows of the service hatch, and the van was ready for business.

A procession of street folk gradually emerged for their soup and coffee. Father Andrew stayed outside the van talking to each and introducing them to Yiska and Nayati, telling them that for a time, they would run the kitchen.

Both boys were well-received by their customers and as the queues thinned out, Yiska and Nayati took a bowl of soup each and sat on the ground with their guests, mingling, starting to build relationships. Father Andrew watched them mix with the homeless people and his confidence grew, the kitchen was in good hands. People who wanted a second bowl or a late arrival interrupted their conversations frequently, but they never seemed to mind.

"I see you Nayati," said a soft, quiet voice suddenly from the shadows.

Nayati smiled with pleasure and replied, "I hear you, Yahzi."

A small figure emerged and stood before him. Her deep brown eyes fixed steadily on his startling blue ones.

105

"It pleases me to see you again, is it food you seek?" he asked her gently, and she nodded her reply, her eyes still fixed on his. He broke the gaze and disappeared into the van, returning quickly with an overflowing bowl of broth, a roll and a cup of coffee. He motioned her to sit down next to Yiska, passed her the food and sat down himself waiting patiently for her to finish her meal.

"You have been well?" Nayati asked Yahzi, when she was sitting drinking her coffee.

"I've not been 'unwell'!" she replied cryptically.

"My brother and I begin to find our way in Muirfield," he tried again. "Where is it that you pass your time?"

"I move around," she replied, looking him in the eye again "I have little to occupy myself, so I like to walk."

"But where do you sleep at night?"

"I sleep where I choose," she replied, not explaining what she meant.

"You would have more soup?" he asked, changing the subject.

She shook her head, "The coffee is good. Another cup would be welcome!"

"I will get more for you," Nayati told her returning to the van.

When he returned, she had gone. Disappeared into the night! Nayati felt a pang of disappointment.

"Did you see where she went Brother?" he asked.

"I was called away briefly and when I returned, she was already gone."

Yiska noticed the disappointment on his brothers face but said nothing.

At two in the morning they closed up the van, leaving the leftover food for replacement the next day. They gathered up and washed the plates and cups and left the rubbish in a trash bin further down the road. Father Andrew left them at the corner of their street with his thanks and a promise to see

106

them the next day, and the boys returned to their new temporary home. Clean towels were on their beds as promised, which reminded Yiska of their task the next morning for Mrs Willoughby. As they lay on their beds, Yiska found himself haunted by the returned memories from earlier that day.

Nayati's thoughts turned to Yahzi, the young girl that he found himself drawn to. He wondered where she came from and how she survived as she did. He would ask Father Andrew about her the next day. It was possible Mrs Willoughby might have met her too, through her work with the church.

Neither boy slept well that night. Even though they had slept in beds the week before, they preferred their sleeping mats and blankets.

As the first rays of the sunrise blessed the forthcoming day the boys were up, pleased to be starting the day early. They showered, enjoying the sensation of water under pressure on their bodies, emerging with their skin tingling.

"It is good to wake this way," Nayati commented and Yiska grinned in confirmation.

They found the exit to the rear garden and left the house. A pile of logs were stacked precariously in one corner of the space, and an axe lay buried in an old stump in front. Nayati pulled it out and tested the sharpness of its cutting edge against his thumb. The boys fell into a routine with one placing a log on the stump whilst the other swung the axe, and it wasn't long before the pile had disappeared.

Yiska pointed to a small lean to that housed the few logs already cut and the two of them stacked the freshly cut ones neatly.

As they finished, Mrs Willoughby came out with a fresh pot of tea and poured them each a cup.

"You two like early starts, don't you?" she said, sitting down with them.

Nayati flashed her his most vibrant smile and replied, "Work is good for the body and the mind."

"I cannot believe that you've done all that so quickly! There is always work. Some tiles on the roof have slipped and need replacing. Perhaps you might do that tomorrow in return for a cooked breakfast?"

"We will be happy to help you with whatever you need," Yiska told her and added with a grin. "Especially for a cooked breakfast!"

"What will you do with yourselves today?" she asked.

"Today I seek someone," Nayati told her.

Yiska looked at him in surprise.

"What about you Yiska?" she asked.

"My brother and I do everything together. I will help him with his search, and we will work at the soup kitchen tonight," Yiska told her.

Mrs Willoughby watched the two boys leave. She was already starting to like having them around!

Chapter 17:
Unfinished Work

They had barely shut Mrs Willoughby's gate when they spotted Father Andrew coming in the opposite direction.

"Morning boys! I'm off to the athletics track for practice. Care to join me?" he asked, in his usual jocular fashion; "competition day is imminent."

"This would be good. There is a matter to discuss," said Nayati, with a serious expression on his face. He turned and started walking alongside, leaving Yiska to follow behind.

"What's on your mind Nayati?" asked the Priest.

"At the kitchen, a girl. She answers to the name Yahzi, I wish to find her," Nayati told him directly.

"I know Yahzi quite well," Father Michael responded. "She's a nice girl; quiet but pleasant. There isn't much to tell though. She began coming to the kitchen two years ago, several times a week. She lives on the streets and sleeps in doorways or on benches in the cemetery.

There was an incident a year ago; the police rescued her after being attacked by drunken teenagers. Strange thing was, they could find no records on her and would have put her into juvenile hall, but she slipped out of the sheriff's office, supposedly to use the bathroom, and disappeared for months. She started turning up at the kitchen again. I could never be sure of her age with her being so short, but I fed her and decided not to report her. She has done no wrong as far as I'm aware, and at least I can monitor her this way."

Nayati thanked him for the information and asked where she was likely to be during the daytime. Father Andrew suggested that the cemetery was a good place to start and gave Nayati directions.

"Brother, I have things to do. I will meet with you later," Nayati told Yiska.

"If you'd like the company, I'll come along with you," suggested Yiska

Nayati shook his head saying, "I will do this alone."

He walked away and Yiska watched him go with a frown on his face.

"I think your brother has taken a liking to this girl," said Father Andrew, with a smile on his face. "The Lord moves in mysterious ways for sure."

Yiska said nothing, but his thoughts were busy. 'Is it possible that my brother thinks about the girl in the same way that I do about Doli? If this is the case, I should help him, as he would help me,' he thought to himself, making his mind up to speak to Nayati about this later.

He was still thinking about it as they turned a corner to see the athletics track in an open space at the end of the street.

There were a group of young people there conducting their warmup rituals trackside. They stopped to wave at Father Andrew as he approached them. He introduced Yiska to them as a fine athlete who had taught the kids in Mason a thing or two on the track. This immediately invited them to challenge Yiska, as Father Andrew knew that it would.

Father Andrew picked a few of the older boys to race against Yiska over the fifteen hundred metre distance and, as he had done in Mason, Yiska removed his shirt and moccasins.

Yiska won the race with consummate ease and the boys crowded around him afterwards to congratulate him.

"How do we compare to the Mason team?" one of them demanded.

Yiska told them that in the interest of fairness he wouldn't answer that. However, he gave some advice on the different tactics that they could use in the race and they appreciated that. He stayed for the duration of the practice helping wherever he could, and by the time he and Father Andrew left, he had made a dozen new friends.

"You are good with people Yiska, young and old alike."

"People need to talk and be listened to."

"That's very philosophical."

"My grandfather says, all need this."

"Sounds like a wise man your grandfather."

"None wiser."

"I hope I get the chance to meet him sometime."

Father Andrew announced that he had to collect some supplies for the youth club, needed for the evening. Usually, the club finished in time for him to attend the soup kitchen; he told Yiska, who was starting to appreciate how hard Father Andrew worked.

Yiska offered his services for a while to help the man out, so Father Andrew led the way back to the church to collect his car.

"Father Michael said that you boys don't travel in cars. Why is this?" he asked.

"It is Nayati who has with a problem with cars. When he was young, a car crash, caused by a hit-and-run driver killed his parents."

"Oh dear, how terrible! The poor boy!" said Father Andrew, shaking his head in disbelief.

They drove to a wholesaler's store and went inside, pushing a trolley down the long aisles. Father Andrew selected a variety of sodas and foodstuff. With the trolley full, they moved to the checkouts. Yiska helped load the trunk of the car and they drove to the small community hall that the youth club operated from.

Father Andrew unlocked the door, and they stepped inside. The hall was more modern than the one in Mason, but the interior layout was similar, with kitchen, games and sitting areas.

Yiska carried in the goods and lay them on the counter. Father Michael told him that he'd been lucky because two of the older members had volunteered to organise the club as they did not want to leave it when they turned eighteen. Without their help, either the soup kitchen or the youth club would have had to close. His last mature kitchen helper had left town six months ago.

After leaving the club, they returned to the church to park the car where Father Andrew announced that he had to see a sick member of his congregation. Yiska left him there and made his way back to Mrs Willoughby's house to meet Nayati.

Chapter 18:
I see you Yahzi

After leaving Father Andrew and his Brother, Nayati made his way down the street carefully following the route the Priest described to him. A while since he'd been alone, he enjoyed the moments of solitude alone with his thoughts. Now and again at home, he would undertake a task that his grandfather set him that gave him a little time away. He always relished the quiet moments that gave him an opportunity to reflect without discussion. The Old Man told him that he inherited the need from him and Nayati was proud to have some of his grandfather's attributes.

He meandered through the streets until the buildings thinned out, and he discerned flat countryside in between them. The road was gradually heading out of town and for a moment Nayati thought that he'd taken a wrong turn. He was about to stop and head back when he spotted a gravestone beyond some metal railings. Relieved, he quickened his pace a little, following the perimeter of the fence until he came upon the two huge metal gates that marked the entrance. Tufts of grass wedged the gates open, showing that the gates were never closed. Nayati passed through.

The gravestones were everywhere he looked. Placed in random spots near the gates but further off in regimented straight lines. It surprised him how large the place was and how many graves it held. If Yahzi was here and wasn't in the open, finding her might take longer than expected. Nayati head towards the middle of the cemetery where a massive old oak tree stood. Intermittent trees were scattered around but none as large as the oak. It took a few minutes to reach it and Nayati saw nobody else on route. Checking he was still alone, Nayati started to climb. Cemeteries were special places; he didn't want to offend anyone. Nobody here though, so up he climbed, higher and higher.

By the time he stopped he was more than thirty feet high, standing on a spot where an ancient branch broke off the previous winter. It left a gap in the foliage and the view of everything around him was clear. He perused the rows of headstones and suddenly an intense sense that he was being watched washed over him. Shivers travelled down his spine, making the hairs on his arms stand on end. He scanned the area like a predator, but nothing gave away the position of somebody else in the graveyard. The sense remained with him as he climbed down. He'd learned long ago to trust his feelings, which often warned of a danger; a mountain lion or rattle snake perhaps, but this time it was different. He was sure; he was being observed by a person.

Back on the ground, he moved to the gates and left. No sooner passing through, the feeling left him, reconfirming his earlier suspicions. He followed the iron fence for a while before he found a gap where three of the metal railings were missing. He slipped through and kept low to conceal his presence behind the stones. Nayati was an excellent tracker and hunter and he slipped into hunting mode moving in total silence between the rows.

He kept this up for fifteen minutes before a sound broke through the silence; a cough that came from just ahead. Somebody, obscured from his view behind a largish stone, sat or crouched, he hoped unaware of his presence. He adjusted his position and started to circle round to get a look at who was there. Soon a pair of legs betrayed the person's

114

position sitting behind the stone. Nayati recognised the clothing.

"I hear you Nayati," a gentle voice called out.

"I see you Yahzi and would tell you that your hearing is good." Nayati said, standing and moving towards her.

She remained seated but smiled as he moved forward and sat in front of her.

"You saw me in the tree, why did you not greet me?"

"At first, I wasn't sure it was you but when I recognised you, I wanted to you to find me. You gave up easily."

"It was my thoughts that you would think I had gone. Like a hunter, I would wait for a sound to show where you are."

"The cough was deliberate so that you would find me. I heard you before I coughed."

"How is this so, I made no sound?"

"When you are homeless and live on the streets, your hearing is important so that you can avoid trouble, especially at night. My hearing is better than most."

"If it keeps you safe, then it is a good thing."

"Why have you come Nayati?"

"It is so that each time I see you there is no time to talk."

"Talk about what?"

"We would talk of many things so that you would know me, and I would know you. We will be as one together."

"Are you saying you like me and want me as your girlfriend?" Yahzi asked with more than a little incredulity.

"My words say what I mean. It is true, I am liking you. I am not understanding of what girlfriend means."

"Do you want to date me then?"

"I have no knowledge of such things."

"Boy! You have a way with words don't you."

"I live far away, and my words are not as yours but when I say that I would talk to you then it is as I say."

Yahzi suddenly smiled. "A conversation with you will not be easy, but what the heck, tell me about yourself Nayati."

For the next two hours Yahzi and Nayati told their stories. Although honest with each other they withheld some information, each held back on details that would expose them more than they were comfortable with.

Both enjoyed the conversation and Yahzi apologised for giving him a hard time at the beginning after admitting that she'd understood what he'd said.

"I have met Navajo that follow the traditional ways before and they speak similar to you, but with a wider vocabulary; most live on the reservation. I learned to speak in the western way because it was expected."

Nayati nodded and fell silent for a moment before continuing.

"It is time for me to seek my brother for we have work tonight."

"At the soup kitchen?"

"Yes! It would be good if you come, we will speak more."

"You would like that?"

"I will learn more of you and this is good."

"Why is this good, you might hear something bad?"

"I do not believe this will be so."

"If I come, we can talk more."

Nayati left her and made his way back to Mrs Willoughby's pleased with the outcome of the day so far.

Chapter 19:
Navajo Magic

Nayati entered his room, followed almost immediately by his brother who also returned.

"How was your day?" Yiska asked.

Nayati sat down on his bed and explained what he'd done.

"I visit to the cemetery to seek Yahzi and, at first, I am not able to find her. There is no other person, but someone watches me while I looked for her. There are tall stones that can hide another; the longer I stayed, the feeling grew that I was not alone.

"Time passed, I left, but return a different way, in the manner of a hunter. I hid behind a tall stone to wait. I wait and wait, then a sound. I move to the sound, Yahzi is behind a stone. She is skilled in ways I did not expect, for she had watched me until I left, yet I saw nothing."

"What did you do then?" Yiska asked him.

"We talk about many things until I return here," Nayati ended, leaving Yiska a little disappointed.

"You like this girl?" Yiska asked, not giving up.

"It is true what you say. She is not as others; she has lived alone for many cycles of the moon, but her smile is as the sun. She will be at the kitchen tonight and we will talk more. You must talk with her too, for I would like your thoughts," Nayati told him.

Yiska nodded, "I will do that for you."

A knock on the door interrupted them.

Yiska opened the door and Mrs Willoughby came in.

"I have your clean clothes," she said, smiling at them. "And, if you can spare some time, I will show you the problem with the roof."

Nayati took the clothes aware of the clean, perfumed smell of them. "I thank you," he said and gave her a broad smile.

She led them outside and pointed to the area where the tiles had become dislodged.

"Little clips position them on the roof," she said.

"There's a ladder that will reach but secure it in place. You boys are up so early I thought it would be better to show you now, especially if you want to finish before breakfast."

"We will finish by then," Nayati assured her.

The day passed gently, before the boys strolled to the soup kitchen. Yiska picked up on the slight spring in his brother's step and smiled, guessing at the reason.

Father Andrew was there with the soup already spluttering in the pot. Steam rose from the kettle and he'd raised the flap that covered the serving hatch; anticipation of the first customers.

"Are we late?" asked Yiska, a little worried.

"No, I'm early for a change!" he told them. "It's a special part of the day for me. This past year I have made many friends here; friends who make you appreciate what you have, because they have so little. Share a coffee with me?" he offered.

"Did you find Yahzi, Nayati?"

"It took time, but I found her. She will be here tonight," he replied.

"She is young to be living on the streets; the youngest that comes here," Father Andrew told him.

"I have thought of seeking her help with the kitchen if you would allow it, but she needs a shower and new clothing first," Nayati pointed out.

"Good idea, but I warn you that she doesn't trust people. As for the clothes and shower, take her to Mrs Willoughby. She met Yahzi when she used to volunteer here, before her arthritis semi-paralysed her," Father Andrew explained.

Nayati looked at him with concern. "She's ill?" he asked.

The Priest recognised Nayati's ignorance of the condition; he explained that she'd suffered a bad bout of arthritis that caused swelling of all her joints and forced her to take to her bed. After finding the right drug to reduce the swelling, she could leave her bed, but she still lives with a lot of pain. The cooler evenings seemed to agitate her condition, which resulted with her no longer helping at the kitchen."

Shadows started moving around the van, so Yiska moved inside to fill the bowls with soup. Nayati followed and tended to the coffee. When the last customer was eating, they came out of the van and mingled with their guests.

Father Andrew admired the ease with which the two chatted with everyone. He liked the way the boys accepted these people without judging them, and he knew that their guests liked them too.

Yahzi made her appearance and Nayati immediately brought food and coffee to give her. She took it, sitting down on the ground. He joined her.

Yiska returned to the kitchen to attend to second helpings, but he monitored the two of them from the van talking and smiling; he was happy for his brother. He joined them later; sitting down next to Yahzi.

119

"It's rare to have the company of two men," she laughed, and Yiska noticed how much more relaxed she seemed.

He joined in with their conversation, forgetting about the kitchen. Father Andrew took over for a while, leaving them to affect Yahzi as they already had him, Mrs Willoughby and his fellow Priest in Mason.

Navajo magic he pondered smiling.

The homeless started to disappear into the shadows and the time to close the kitchen had arrived.

Nayati used all his persuasive skills to tempt Yahzi to visit Mrs Willoughby's for a shower, even though he hadn't asked her permission. He was confident she would agree; as he'd already woven his charm on her, and she already doted on him. To his surprise, he realised he'd formed an attachment to her too.

Nayati was enjoying his time in Muirfield and was looking forward to each day's adventure, but Yiska was not enjoying the same sense of excitement. Close to finding what most people already knew about themselves, his patience was wearing thin. He'd waited a long time for answers and now the anticipation was becoming unbearable. Not his normal self; he felt irritable and, even though he understood the reasons, he couldn't relax.

Chapter 20:
Seen One, Seem Them All

At first light, the two boys left their beds and attended to Mrs Willoughby's roof. The task was straightforward and took them less than an hour. They showered and put on the clean clothes Mrs Willoughby had laundered for them. A knock at the door and Mrs Willoughby entered when Yiska opened it.

"Good morning, boys! Breakfast is in ten minutes," she said, straightening the roughly opened curtains. Dirty clothes lay in a heap on the beds and she picked them up.

"I'll be taking these clothes too; Roof work is such a dirty job!"

Nayati gave her his best smile as she walked out of the room, and she could not help but return it. Ten minutes later, she called them into the kitchen.

"Eggs, bacon, sausages, beans and fresh bread," she told them, smiling. "I've not cooked a breakfast like this in ages - so eat up and enjoy it!"

Once more Nayati struggled with his knife and fork and, as he attempted to spear a sausage with his fork, it shot off his plate and onto the table.

Mrs Willoughby apologised saying that she had fried the sausages in corn oil, so they had a tendency to be a little slippery.

121

Yiska feigned a coughing fit to disguise a laugh, but secretly pleased she had spared his brother from embarrassment.

She showed Nayati how to hold the utensils and smiled as he attempted to master it.

"You have knowledge of Yahzi, the girl who lives with no home?" Nayati asked.

"Yahzi is a lovely girl, not a bad bone in her body! Sometimes, when times are hard, street people do bad things to help them survive, like stealing, but Yahzi, to my knowledge, has never done this. How she survives is a mystery to me! When I worked in the soup kitchen, she only came two or three times a week, but unlike many, she always had a friendly word for the helpers. She doesn't seem to mix much with the other street people, probably because she's so much younger than them, so keeps herself to herself.

"She spends a lot of time in the cemetery; sleeps there too. I offered her a room here once, to get herself sorted out, but she said she preferred the outdoors. My guess is that she has something in her past to hide; something unpleasant. There, that's about it, why do you ask?"

"I wish to help her. She needs the shower and clean clothes. I would seek your agreement to bring her here to clean."

Mrs Willoughby smiled at his turn of phrase. "You like this girl, don't you?"

Nayati nodded.

"If you can persuade her to come, she can shower, and I have old clothes, from when I was young, in the attic."

"I am in your debt again," Nayati told her.

"Nonsense! You're trying to help somebody, that's a lovely thing to do," she told him.

"I'm going to the track to help Father Andrew again today. There's only three days left till the track meeting with Mason, and his team needs help. I guess that you'll be sorting out things with Yahzi, so we'll meet up later, back here this afternoon," Yiska told his brother.

Nayati nodded his agreement and the two of them headed outside after thanking Mrs Willoughby for their meal.

They separated, with Nayati heading for the cemetery. As he left the main part of the town, the cry of an eagle sounded, and he looked up to watch his animal spirit circling above. A pang of worry coursed through him; the bird called only when something was wrong.

Behind, he spotted a black and white car with flashing lights on the roof, making its way down the road. A little way ahead of him, an old woman was sitting on a bench, a paper sack of groceries at her feet. As nothing seemed untoward, it left Nayati with a vague sense of unease, especially as his totem was reliable.

He reached the bench, recognising the woman as the next-door neighbour of Mrs Willoughby, and greeted her. Meanwhile, the car caught up with him and slowed, the nearside window opening. A man in a light tan uniform ordered him to stop. Nayati did as told and waited whilst the man got out of his vehicle and approached him.

He towered a full six inches above Nayati and glared down at him with hostile, grey eyes. His mouth hid in the coarse, sandy tangle of his beard, but advancing middle age had caused his hair to recede on top of his head, leaving just enough to comb on either side.

"Watcha doing out here, boy?" he drawled, revealing yellow stained teeth through the hole in his beard.

"I am walking," said Nayati calmly.

"Where to, boy?" the man persisted.

"Down there," Nayati pointed.

"I've not seen you around here before. What's your name?"

"I am Nayati."

"Nayati what?"

"I am Nayati."

123

"Don't sass me, boy. What's your last name?" he asked, drawing a large stick out from his belt and pointing it at Nayati's face.

"I am Nayati of the Navajo," answered Nayati, which seemed to irritate the man.

"Where do you live, boy?" he asked, lowering his stick and resting it on Nayati's chest.

"I live with Mrs Willoughby,"

"Address?"

"I do not wear a dress; I am a man" Nayati responded.

"I warned you already about sassing me, boy. Where do you work?" he snapped, pushing the stick harder into Nayati's chest.

Nayati stood firm against the pressure and then said, "I do God's work."

With this the man lost his temper, took his gun from a holster on his belt and pointed it at Nayati. "Hands up, lean on the car."

Nayati raised his hands but remained where he stood.

The man shoved him against the car. He kicked his legs apart and forced one of Nayati's arms behind his body. Nayati started to resist, but his strength was no match for this man. Something cold wrapped around his wrist, before his other hand, forced behind his back, received the same treatment and he could no longer separate his arms. The man wrenched open the rear door of the car and pushed Nayati inside; the door slammed behind him.

As they drove away, the old lady on the bench rose from her seat and walked back towards town with an angry, but determined, look on her face.

Driven to the Sheriff's department, the man yanked out Nayati and marched him into an office and forced him to sit in a chair.

"Watcha got, Deputy Williams?" a voice from across the room asked.

"Just a sassy Indian who I'm arresting for vagrancy and resisting arrest, Sheriff," he told the smaller man with intelligent eyes, as he left his seat and approached them.

"Won't give me a name or an address and says he's 'doing God's work'," he continued.

"Leave him to stew for a while; that always makes them more cooperative," he said. Then as if to give Nayati a chance, the sheriff asked him what his name was.

Nayati replied in the same calm manner that had so irked the deputy, "I answer this already, but my answer is not believed."

The sheriff turned away, moving back to his desk, whilst the deputy exited the room. Nayati sat, ignoring the discomfort of his cuffed hands. After about twenty minutes, a commotion erupted outside. A woman's voice agitated and shrill, and the deputy's voice doing his best to calm her down. The door burst open and a furious Mrs Willoughby stormed the office, followed by the deputy and the woman who had witnessed everything.

The sheriff stood and hurried over towards them.

"What's going on here?" he demanded.

"Don't you ask me those darn silly questions, Sheriff Briggs? What have you done with my boy?" she snapped and then caught sight of Nayati sitting on his chair in handcuffs.

"Take those things off of him. Now!" she raged.

"Are you all right, Nayati?"

"I find these things uncomfortable, but I am good, Mrs Willoughby," responded Nayati gently.

Sheriff Briggs took over. "Mrs Willoughby, please calm down and take a seat. Let's try to sort this out," he said.

"There is nothing to sort out. I aware of what happened and there is a witness. Take those handcuffs off my boy," she snapped.

Sheriff Briggs nodded to his deputy, who moved across to Nayati and removed the cuffs.

"Bring him over here," he commanded. He motioned for Nayati to sit and Mrs Willoughby immediately sat down beside him.

The deputy brought another chair for her friend and the sheriff sat down behind his desk, scratching his head, whilst the deputy took position behind Nayati.

"Now what is going on?" he asked.

"I want your deputy charged with harassment, that's what!" said Mrs Willoughby in a calmer voice. "He provoked my boy here and then arrested him on trumped-up charges."

"Deputy?" invited the sheriff, his eyebrows raised in question. "Would you care to explain?"

"I was driving down Main Street when I spotted a boy, I hadn't seen him before, so I stopped to find out who he was. I asked him his name, and he told me, 'Nayati'. When I asked for his last name, he told me that he was Nayati of the Navajo, so I warned him about sassing the law. Then I asked him where he lived and said at this lady's house. I asked him for his address, but he told me that he had no dress. I asked him where he worked, and he told me that he did God's work. With that and refusing to answer my questions, I had no option but to arrest him."

"He answered those questions," Mrs Willoughby blurted. "Is your deputy so dense that he didn't notice that Nayati's not from round here and his understanding of English is incomplete?"

The deputy squirmed at the insult, but the sheriff came to his rescue.

"Mrs Willoughby, please do not insult an officer doing his duty," he admonished. "Deputy, care to comment here?"

"I must admit I didn't notice that the boy had a language problem. He seemed to answer my questions as if he understood them all right."

"And the dress comment?" pursued the sheriff.

"I thought he was being sassy," he answered.

"Well, misunderstanding on both parts," said the sheriff, trying to find a common ground.

"The only mistake Nayati made, is not understanding the English language," interrupted Mrs Willoughby.

"It appears so," the sheriff conceded. "Before I release him into your care though, what is 'God's work' that he does?"

"He works at Father Andrew's soup kitchen every night and does a lot of good work to help lonely old people like me. God's work!"

The Sheriff nodded and told them that Nayati was free to go. He held out his hand to Nayati to show there was no ill-will, and Nayati shook it.

"Deputy!" said the Sheriff, and he too held out his hand for Nayati to shake.

"That shouldn't have happened!" Are you sure you're all right? You were lucky that Mrs Baker witnessed what happened and came to tell me," said Mrs Willoughby.

"I am good," Nayati told her "And I am in your debt again, and your neighbour."

"Let's get you home and get a nice cup of tea," she continued.

"I thank you, but I still must find Yahzi, for she needs our help, too," Nayati told her.

"Oh, silly me! I forgot that was where you were heading off to. I'll tell you what... Why don't I come with you, just to make sure you don't get arrested again?"

Nayati smiled. "It would please me to have your company."

They said goodbye to Mrs Baker, showering her with gratitude as they turned in the cemetery's direction.

Chapter 21:
A Mother's Instinct

"Mrs Willoughby, you walk as if you are in great danger!"

"What, what do you mean?"

"You walk fast."

"Oh, I'm sorry, is it too quick for you."

"There is no need."

"I'm still angry from before, now we're on a mission. Sometimes I just can't help myself."

"Yahzi is there, of this I am sure."

"You're right."

"If we walk like this, we will miss seeing what is here."

"What do you mean?"

"A rabbit hides in that bush."

"Where, I can't see it?"

"It moved there as we got closer."

"Are you playing a trick on me?"

Nayati picked up a small pebble and threw it to the left of the bush but close enough to make a dull thud that surprised the rabbit. It left at speed with its tail bobbing up and down.

"Well, I'll be a... You're right! I love seeing rabbits. What else have I missed?"

"The tree there. The lower branch. What do you see?"

"Nothing, nothing at all. No! Wait! There's an owl sitting there, a big one. I hear them sometimes but never see one."

"When you understand of the creatures, finding them is easy." Nayati told her grinning.

"I declare, you two boys are a constant surprise."

Their walk continued and Nayati pointed out a few plants used for flavourings or medicinal purposes.

"Who taught you about all this Nayati?"

"I learned much from my grandfather, but he says that we can learn from all people and he is right. I learn from Yiska and I learn from Doli my sister. She is good at all things."

"How old is she?"

"We entered the world of men together."

"You're twins!"

"Yes."

"You must miss her, there's a special bond between twins. Are you identical?"

"I miss her presence; we are not apart before this journey. I do not understand the other word."

"Identical means the same. Do you look alike?"

"We are the same in our looks but not in our ways. Yiska misses her. They are as one together."

"You mean they are boyfriend and girlfriend?"

"Is this not what I said."

"You speak in such an unusual way Nayati, it's not the same as Yiska."

"This is true. I grow in the ways of the Navajo and Yiska is still learning our ways. He learns quick."

"You complement each other very well; I mean you are good together."

"We are brothers for four autumns."

They approached the cemetery and passed through the iron gates. Mrs Willoughby quietened.

"Are you knowing of the spirits here?"

"I'm getting older Nayati and as I age, more of the people I once knew rest here."

"Do you visit the stones and talk to them?"

"Sometimes just being here is enough. You don't speak to the stones."

"This I understand, you speak to the spirits of those who have gone."

"Yes."

"Why do they visit this place?"

"A cemetery is the meeting place for the physical and spiritual worlds. Some say it is the church that fills this purpose, but it is my belief that you can talk to God or those who has died anywhere."

"My grandfather visits the desert each autumn to be with the spirit of my grandmother."

"Do you seek the company of your grandmother Nayati?"

"I did not see my grandmother but I know much about her. Niyol tells her smile is like the rising of the sun and Doli has the same smile."

"That's beautiful."

"We say things are like from the world. We can see what is not there."

"That's very romantic, the girls will love you."

"I need no girls but Yahzi is good."

"Yahzi is a girl."

"Yahzi is more, she has knowledge others do not. She survives without a home."

"You're saying that she is mature Nayati. Do you like the way she looks?"

"She is to my liking."

"Do you like the way she speaks?"

"It is to my liking."

"Does she make you feel something deep inside?"

"How is it that you have knowledge of this, it is not seen?"

"This is how your brother feels about Doli. It's called love."

They moved deeper into the cemetery and Nayati led Mrs Willoughby to the place where Yahzi had sat the day before, but she wasn't there.

"Oh dear, we might be wrong about her being here."

"We are not wrong she is watching us."

Mrs Willoughby made no attempt to ask Nayati what he meant. She didn't doubt what he said. Nayati moved off again, and she followed. Nayati moved across several rows of stones and stopped short of one.

"A person should greet those who come to visit."

From behind the stone Yahzi rose and stood to face him.

"How did you find me; I didn't make a sound?"

"The nose of a hunter, there is food that I could smell."

Yahzi smiled. "Well, you're quite the hunter."

"I bring a friend to greet you."

"Hello Mrs Willoughby, your health is better than the last time I saw you."

"It is Yahzi, how are you, I haven't seen you since I stopped working at the soup kitchen."

"I'm well thank you? why the visit?"

"Would you mind if we sit down on a bench my dear,

I find it easy enough to sit down on the ground but very painful getting up again."

They sat down on the closest bench, Yahzi sitting next to the old woman. Nayati moved to sit the other side of her but Mrs Willoughby raised her hand to stop him.

"Nayati would you do an old woman a kindness and buy me a drink from the shop down the street. Perhaps you could get one for yourself and one for Yahzi too."

"You walk too far, there is pain?"

"You are such a thoughtful young man. No, nothing like that Nayati, I'm just thirsty."

She offered coins to Nayati, who refused them saying he had coins of his own. He walked off after telling her that he wouldn't be long.

Yahzi looked at Mrs Willoughby and studied her face.

"You aren't thirsty, are you?"

"Sometimes it's easier for women to talk if there are no men around."

Yahzi laughed. "What's on your mind?"

"Ooh! How about second chances, life, love, woman's stuff."

Yahzi remained quiet and Mrs Willoughby took the chance.

"I will talk to you very directly and I hope anything I say will not offend you. When you used to visit the soup kitchen, that is when I worked there, I always had an inkling that you differed from the other homeless people. I didn't know why and still don't, and in truth it doesn't matter. I guess to sum it all up I always believed you were a good person. How you ended up on the streets is a mystery but I'm here to offer you a chance to leave this life. You are too young for this; your whole life is ahead of you; you just don't deserve this."

"But I am nobody to you?"

"You are not nobody Yahzi, I try very hard to live my life in a Christian way and at the very least that is reason enough. No young girl, should be on the streets."

"What if I told you that I chose to be on the streets, would that change your opinion of me?"

"I can't begin to imagine why you would do that, but it changes nothing."

"It is true, I chose this life because of the past, and I don't want to talk about that."

132

"The past is the past, it's not now. If I said you could have a room of your own, and a job to pay your way, would you be interested?"

"It is time for me to leave this life, but in truth, it is easier becoming a street person than to stop being one."

"Thinking like this is a positive step."

"Why now, why today, yesterday or the day before?"

"I met and made two new friends who remind me, by their actions and thoughts, that there are still some decent people in the world, and that I am duty bound to help anybody that needs it. Between them they have nothing and yet they are richer than most people."

"The two you speak of are Nayati and Yiska?"

"That's right and one of them cares for you."

"I like him a lot too." Yahzi blurted, blushing.

"He is worth changing the way you live for?"

"He might be."

"Return with us and live again."

Nayati returned with three bottles of coke. He handed one to each of the women before unscrewing the top of his own. Mrs Willoughby looked at it with apprehension. Yahzi drank, and as Mrs Willoughby hadn't attempted to open hers Nayati did it for her.

"Drink, it is good," he told her smiling. She took a sip and nodded and inadvertently burped.

"Whoops," she said smiling, as the others laughed.

They drank slowly and enjoyed the sunshine and the peace before Mrs Willoughby broke the silence.

"Yahzi has something to tell you Nayati."

"What is it you wish to say Yahzi?"

"I am changing the way I live, and Mrs Willoughby has provided me with an opportunity too good to miss."

"What is this opportunity?"

"I am coming back with you."

"Today is a good day. Nayati said, giving Yahzi a smile that could melt a polar ice cap."

133

Chapter 22:
Eagle Rescue

Yiska strolled towards the athletics track. Far too early for practice, he had time to pass and spent some time browsing in the shop windows.

Many of the shopkeepers were only just opening their doors and bid him good morning as he passed. He responded but didn't stop to talk; a minestrone of worries in the soup of his mind. The knowledge of indiscriminate failings in his past contradicted the person he'd become. The heaviness consumed him, and his shoulders sagged under its weight as he wandered down the street.

He could discuss everything with Father Michael when they met again at the athletics meet in two days' time. He liked and trusted Father Andrew, but for reasons he wasn't sure about, he felt more comfortable about sharing his personal problems with Father Michael.

At the track, he sat down in one of the small viewing stands, overlooking the field. *Maybe I should talk to the two of them together; they're both used to troubled people, he mused.* The worry about discussing the past with such good men weighed heavy, and negative thoughts whirled around the chaos of his mind adding to his confusion.

He sat in silent conflict for some time before realising he was not alone. The cry of his eagle captured his attention, and he searched for the trouble that soften followed its cry.

A group of six youths ambled towards him. At first it didn't worry him, but he wondered why the eagle had called out. He watched the group approach and apprehension coursed through him when they silently formed a circle around him.

The tallest spoke. "You are in my seat," he said, staccato, with a sneer on his face. "I don't like it when an Injun sits in my seat."

Yiska remained calm and civil. "I didn't realise this was your seat. Here, you can have it!" he replied, standing up.

"Don't want it now an Injun's sat on it. That's gonna cost ya."

"There is a charge for sitting here?" Yiska enquired.

"Sure is Injun boy. Ain't that right, boys?" he asked his companions, who sniggered their agreement.

"What's the cost?" Yiska asked.

"Ten dollars and a good beating, for a start," the threat in his voice intensifying.

"I don't have ten dollars with me, and I don't want to beat anybody," said Yiska responded, flippantly.

"Quick with the humour ain't you, Injun? Let's see how you like this then…" He raised his fist and drew it back.

Yiska read his intention and prepared himself.

As the youth propelled his fist towards Yiska's face, Yiska's arm moved up at lightning speed, catching it in his hand. He locked his elbow out straight and gripped the clenched fist firmly. Looking the youth straight in the eye, he said, "Leave it! You do not want to do this."

"Oh yes, I do!" said the youth, kicking out with his left leg.

Yiska caught it in his other hand and raised it high enough to make his assailant fall over backwards. This had an instant effect on the youth who ordered the others to get him. With five grown youths attacking at once, it was easy for them to knock Yiska to the ground. Two of them pinned his arms down and two, his legs.

The leader was back on his feet and standing over Yiska, the anger and humiliation showing on his face.

"You're gonna pay for that, big time," he spat. "Any last requests, Injun?"

"Just one," answered Yiska calmly. "Duck!"

"What d'ya mean, duck?" the leader asked, in confusion.

Yiska gestured sideways with his head. "It's an instruction–duck!"

The eagle had made its descent quietly, until it changed to a diving mode. It tore through the air at break-neck speed at the boy who stood over Yiska. As the whistling sound of the bird's strained feathers reached his ears, he turned in time to register his plight. Ducking, the great bird shrieked past him with inches to spare, shrieking out its call as it did so.

Yiska watched the bird pass, rising into the air once more and wheeling round. It would come again.

The boys holding him down released their grip and started to get up, but they were slow and were forced to throw themselves down to the ground again as the bird swooped down, as close as the first time. Recovering faster than the others and standing up, Yiska smiled his thanks at the bird.

The other youths began to circle him once more as a familiar voice reached Yiska.

"What's going on here? Beat it, before I call the police."

"Who's gonna make me, you old man?" the leader taunted.

"I will, If I have to," said Father Andrew.

"And I will," said another voice.

"And me!"

"Me too!"

Yiska looked behind Father Andrew and saw several members of the athletics club arriving. "The numbers are a little fairer now," he suggested. "Still want to play?"

Some gang members were already melting into the background, not liking their lack of advantage.

The leader scowled at Yiska, "this ain't finished."

Then he turned and followed his group across the field.

"Your timing was perfect, Father Andrew," said Yiska grinning. "Thank you, all of you!"

The group of boys gathered around him, patting him on the back like they would a hero.

"I saw what that bird did! I've seen nothing like that in my life!" Father Andrew told him.

"It is my animal spirit. It has been with me since the desert," Yiska told him proudly.

"I would say the bird acts for God! But, whatever... It favours you. Are you hurt at all?" Father Andrew asked.

"No, I'm fine. They never got around to hitting me," Yiska answered.

"In that case, keep your eyes and ears open for any more signs of trouble, but it's time to practise. It's only two days now till the meet," said Father Andrew. "Get yourselves warmed up," he ordered.

While the athletes undertook a variety of jogging and stretching activities, Father Andrew asked Yiska what had happened. On hearing Yiska's account, Father Andrew told him that it wasn't an isolated incident. The boys couldn't find work, there was nothing for them. Unable to fill their time, they hung around displaying threatening behaviour and creating trouble. They were in constant conflict with the police and been arrested many times for petty crimes.

Yiska helped Father Andrew at the track for the rest of the morning and walked back part of the way with him to Mrs Willoughby's. He let himself in and went to his room, noticing that nobody else was home. He was not expecting Nayati to be there, though he wished he was; but Mrs Willoughby might have been. Aware that Father Andrew had asked her to help find out about his parents, he was hoping to ask her what she'd found out so far.

He lay down on his bed, suddenly experiencing loneliness. How he wished Doli were here! She always made him feel good about himself, about life; in fact, just about everything! He formed images of her in his mind; her long dark hair, the deep blue eyes that seemed to swallow him and the dazzling smile that he could never resist.

Doli's serene face faded into the cragginess of Niyol, the ancient Navajo who'd had such a strong influence on his life with an amazing knack of seeing the world in a simple, yet profound way. *How does he do that? he asked himself. Everything seems clear to him!* He let himself doze and then the bliss of sleep relieved him of his melancholy.

Nayati entered the room after a short while later, surprised to find his brother asleep.

Yiska woke immediately and grinned at him. "Did you find her?" he asked.

"I did. Mrs Willoughby says we must stay in here until called!"

"We are? Why is that?" asked Yiska, his curiosity getting the better of him.

"Mrs Willoughby attends to the needs of Yahzi," said Nayati.

"What needs?"

"She is becoming clean and will soon receive a gift of clothes!"

"Oh, now I understand!" Yiska answered.

"How was your day, Brother?" asked Nayati.

"Different," Yiska told him. "But I will tell you about it later."

An hour passed, then a knock at the door.

Mrs Willoughby led them through to the living area. "Wait here!" she instructed leaving the room.

Yiska looked at Nayati and shrugged.

Mrs Willoughby entered again. "Boys, we have a new guest!" she said smiling. "Allow me to introduce you to Yahzi."

Nayati's mouth dropped open in surprise and delight as Yahzi entered. She was clean, with her long dark hair straight and combed. She was wearing a simple, white, western-style cotton dress that contrasted her dark skin. Nayati stared at her transformation.

"Nayati, it's rude to stare," Mrs Willoughby told him, a wide smile breaking across her face. She realised the effect this vision in front of him was having.

"You are as the sunset on a summer's day," he said, lapsing into silence once more, unable to take his eyes off her.

Yahzi blushed, before thanking him for the compliment in her gentle voice.

Yiska came to his brother's aid. "You are as beautiful as my brother says," he told her. "I cannot believe that you are the same girl who shared a meal with us at the diner the other night. Mrs Willoughby is there no end to your talents?"

"You can hide what lies underneath, but you cannot change what is there dear!" she said, delighted at the boys' responses to Yahzi.

"How do you feel, Yahzi?" Yiska asked her.

"These are strange clothes for me to wear, but I find them pleasant. It's good to be clean, too!" she said with a bashful smile.

"I would walk with you a while. You will come?" Nayati asked her.

139

Yahzi nodded, and Mrs Willoughby and Yiska watched them walk down the short path, pass through the white picket gate and stroll down the street.

Mrs Willoughby suggested coffee, which Yiska accepted.

"Are you aware of the effect you and your brother have on people?" she asked.

"What effect?"

"Let me tell you then! You make people smile and spread happiness; you touch people with your ways. And that's a good thing," she added, laughing at his ignorance of it.

A knock at the door announced Father Andrew's arrival, escorted in by Mrs Willoughby.

"My, we are busy today! Join us in a coffee?" she offered, pleased when he accepted. "To what do I owe the pleasure of this visit?" she asked the Priest.

"Well, it's the strangest thing, but I've just seen Nayati walking down the road with a most beautiful, young lady. I'm convinced the young lady was none other than our young friend, Yahzi. Mrs Willoughby, you've been weaving your magic again, haven't you?"

Mrs Willoughby flushed with delight at the unexpected praise but dismissed it.

"It is these two boys who weave magic. They make everyone they touch smile." she smiled.

"Including you?" he suggested.

"And you," she countered.

"There is much to be thankful for, then!" he said, raising his cup towards Yiska.

Chapter 23:
Eagle Spirits

Nayati and Yahzi returned and a party atmosphere at Mrs Willoughby's developed. Father Andrew started to tell them about Yiska's incident at the track, describing in detail about the youth who tried to hit Yiska and the eagle swooping down to defend him.

"I'm sure the way Yiska defended himself suggests he's had some training. Fortunate, considering," Father Andrew told them.

Yiska wasn't so comfortable about it and hadn't given a thought to his experience of fighting, he believed he'd just acted on reflex. Another worry, adding to growing concerns about his past life and exploits.

Nayati spoke out. "How is this so, the eagle saved Yiska and it was also with me? It warned of the trouble that found me," he said. "I do not understand this."

"Trouble, what trouble?" asked Yiska, concern clear on his face.

Nayati explained that, on his way to meet Yahzi, a deputy stopped him. Mrs Willoughby took over from there. She also was a good storyteller and omitted no details. They all laughed at Nayati's confusion with address/a dress, but he still looked confused. Yahzi explained what an address was and Nayati realised his mistake.

"It is no surprise that the deputy did not like my answer," he said, joining in with the laughter.

Mrs Willoughby continued the story, explaining how her friend Mrs Baker had witnessed the whole thing and, recognising Nayati, informed her.

"Silly man lacks the brains to be a deputy. I can tell you that I gave the sheriff and the deputy a piece of my mind. Pah! Arrest my boy! Not while I'm around."

Nayati interrupted her flow. "I was sitting in the sheriff's office when I heard a noise like a storm. The deputy is this high," he showed a height six inches above his head. "Mrs Willoughby is this high," he said, pointing to his chest. "The big man was no match for Mrs Willoughby. She needed no stick or gun, just the words she spoke, with the speed of a mountain cat." They all laughed at this. "When I left the office, the eagle was still above my head," Nayati stated.

Mrs Willoughby asked them about the eagles, and the boys realised that she and Yahzi knew nothing about their spirit animals. Describing how they came to have eagles as their guides, he left out some of the details, but explained the principles behind the Navajo beliefs.

Father Andrew suggested that God sent them to protect the boys, and Yiska said that he understood why Father Andrew believed that.

Mrs Willoughby was more open-minded. "Plenty of religions and a place for each," she stated emphatically, "providing their teachings encourage people to care, and improve the world."

"Well said, Mrs Willoughby!" commented Father Andrew. "Amen to that."

Nayati then asked, "There were two eagles? We have only ever seen one."

"I might be able to explain that," said Father Andrew. "In the Catholic religion, we have the Holy Spirit which can reach out and touch many people at one time. If your eagle is a spirit, why shouldn't it reach out and touch more than one person at the same time?"

Nayati liked the explanation and was at ease with it.

"I will discuss this with Niyol when I am home. It is my thoughts that he will agree. You are most wise, Father Andrew."

The Priest nodded, pleased with the way Nayati had responded.

"So, Yahzi," Mrs Willoughby said, changing the subject. "Now that you are clean, well-dressed and amongst friends, what's it like to have a roof over your head again and know that you'll sleep in a bed tonight?"

Yahzi looked suddenly shocked. "I will sleep where I always sleep, out in the open," she answered quickly.

"Mrs Baker next door has a spare room. I have asked her if she would let you use it," said the woman gently.

"Thank you, but there is no need. Shut in a room would be horrible," Yahzi told her.

Father Andrew suddenly put two and two together. "Yahzi, did you once go to the orphanage?" he asked.

At first, Yahzi didn't answer but then she confirmed this with a nod.

"I escaped from there before they closed it down. It was awful, and the owners were horrible. They did terrible things and they hurt you if you didn't do as they asked. They locked me in a storeroom for days once and I was beaten many times."

Father Andrew revealed his awareness of bad things that occurred there, and his belief that they could not hold the children accountable. He understood Yahzi's reasons and made another suggestion.

"Mrs Willoughby! You have a porch with a swing seat. Why don't you let Yahzi sleep there? She will be safe there and she won't be in a room. Would that be all right Yahzi?" he asked.

"It's better" she said. I would like to pay my way. I don't have money, but I can work."

"We can sort that out later," Mrs Willoughby said quickly.

"Why don't you come to the soup kitchen with us tonight? You know everybody that comes along," Father Andrew suggested.

"I will come with Nayati."

Yahzi's admission to attending the orphanage had stunned Yiska to silence. He looked hard at her, trying to remember her face, unaware that he was staring so hard that the others had noticed and stopped talking.

"Yahzi, you were at the orphanage; I was there too! Did you know me there?" Yiska asked. To his amazement, she nodded.

"Your name is David, but you call yourself Yiska?"

Yiska shook his head in relief. At last he'd met someone from the orphanage.

"You said nothing, why?" he asked.

"I live on the streets to forget who and what I was. I tried to change into the person you know. It has taken all this time. I thought when you left, you'd been doing the same," she told him.

"Yiska, why don't you start at the beginning and tell her what happened to you," Father Andrew suggested.

Yiska nodded and started from the time Niyol found in the desert. He did not elaborate on the details, nor did he describe his home, but brought the story up to the present.

"Whatever you remember about me at the orphanage would be a great help." Yiska pleaded.

"I will tell you what I remember, but it will not help you and it will weigh on your mind." Yahzi told him. "They sent me to the orphanage before you came, a few weeks. You were quiet and kept yourself to yourself and you made no friends. Because you were small like me, they took you out to help in robberies. At first you went through dog flaps, as I

144

did. Then, as you grew, they used you to get in through small windows. When you were older, they took you inside the houses to steal. You refused and were badly beaten and starved, this was the punishment for anyone who refused. You refused many times and suffered the same fate until one day you disappeared, and I never saw you again until the diner.

As far as I can remember you never made a single friend in all the time you were there, but you were kind with the younger children, and they liked you. You were good to me too. Once, when I was in the laundry room, they beat me because a bird messed on a pair of the owner's trousers when they hung outside. You comforted me even though you were no older than me. Sometimes you comforted others too!

But you are part Indian and part American and because of this they treated you worse. They used you as slaves to other older groups and they would steal your food. When you disappeared, I suspected they had beaten you to death. Many disappeared. It was a horrible life with horrible people," she told them.

Father Andrew spoke next. "It would appear Yiska that you didn't have any involvement in stealing after you realised it was wrong, despite the suffering you endured. As a minor, you've displayed tremendous courage and have a fine sense of what's right and wrong."

"I still got into the houses and let them in though," said Yiska, his disgust at what he did obvious.

"You were just five or six years old, Yiska! We cannot blame you for that. You didn't even understand what you were doing, other than doing what the grown-ups told you to," said Mrs Willoughby added.

"It doesn't change what I did," Yiska said with shame. "Yahzi, how do you feel about what they made us to do?"

145

"The same as you, Yiska. My punishment was to be homeless for three years. I have done nothing bad and refused help many times because of the shame. It has not been easy."

"Why so long?" asked Yiska.

"One year for each of the years I helped them in their robberies."

"That's why you were ready to make a change, dear?" asked Mrs Willoughby.

"I have completed the punishment I gave myself, and I have met Nayati. He would not want a girl who is filthy and lives on the street," she answered.

"I did!" said Nayati, responding to her reasoning. "It was the person you are that is important not where you lived."

She smiled, and he returned it.

Yiska thanked her for sharing and reliving her horrors.

"Watching you refuse to help them, and being beaten time and time again, gave me the courage to follow your example," she stated.

Father Andrew left, saying that he would see them at the soup kitchen, but Mrs Willoughby stayed, talking and laughing with them. It had been many years since she'd experienced family life and was enjoying it. The fondness for the young people in her company was clear, and she was proud of her association with them. She headed into the kitchen to bake some biscuits; humming a hymn as she worked. She felt like a mother again! She enjoyed herself so much, that after the three of them left for the soup kitchen, she experienced feelings of loneliness.

Father Andrew arrived early at the soup kitchen. Like Mrs Willoughby, he enjoyed the company of the boys; he would enjoy getting to know Yahzi better too. Many people that could learn life lessons from them and he wished he could bottle what they had and sprinkle it during Holy

Communion! The additional time he could spend mixing with the homeless people, because of their help, was invaluable in making progress with these troubled individuals.

Two men were close to leaving the streets, and with patience he might persuade more to follow. Nayati and Yiska could focus on the younger homeless people, and with Yahzi, well anything might happen! The boys gave him so much more than help and time; they'd given him a renewed sense of hope.

Yahzi was a revelation that night. She spent the whole evening talking to the homeless people. Her transformation amazed them. She commanded the attention of a large group of them and, for a time, there was almost a party mood. Although the soup kitchen closed at the normal time, the homeless stayed for longer, before Father Andrew said they had better go, before they all got arrested for loitering!

They left, tired, but pleased with their night's work.

Chapter 24:
Orphanage Life

Nayati and Yiska were up at first light and moved outside to assess the day.

"Yahzi has gone," Nayati stated the obvious, as he looked at the empty swing. Blankets sat on it, folded, but there was no sign of the girl anywhere. Yiska noticed a slight note of concern in Nayati's voice and explained that she had gone for an early walk or something.

"Nayati I wanted to ask you something."

"What is it that you need Brother?"

"I want to talk to Yahzi about the time we spent at the orphanage. I sensed last night that she didn't really want to talk about it, but I have to discover whatever I can. Would you encourage her to talk to me?"

"This matter is painful for you and it is painful for Yahzi. It is my thoughts that this is something only you can discuss with Yahzi. Many would not understand the feelings you have. This makes it hard to talk about. You understand and she understands. Ask her, if she says yes, then talk to her alone. If she says no, then I will ask for you. This is good with you?"

"You sound more and more like Niyol these days Brother."

"If that is true, it is good."

"It is true, and it is good!"

Just then the gate opened at the back of the yard and Yahzi walked in holding a bunch of wildflowers.

"I was wondering when you two would get up," she said smiling.

"We are awake at first light, but you rise before this."

"I wanted to get some flowers for Mrs Willoughby as a thank you for yesterday."

"She will love them," Yiska told her.

"What are your plans for today," she asked them.

"We will help Father Andrew at the track, but we have some time before we need to leave for there. Mrs Willoughby will cook us breakfast soon; It's good and you'll enjoy it."

At that moment Mrs Willoughby walked out into the early sunshine.

"I heard you talking, did you sleep well Yahzi? Oh, what lovely flowers."

"I slept fine and the flowers are for you, a thank you for your kindness."

She picked them up and held them to her nose. "They smell beautiful, how thoughtful of you Yahzi. Right! Breakfasts all round after you've all showered."

After breakfast Yiska approached Yahzi. He looked and felt uneasy, but he had to ask.

"Yahzi there is something I have to ask you about and, it's just..."

"You want to know what I remember from the orphanage. I will tell you what I can, but it might not be enough to ease how you feel about it and yourself."

"The drink with bubbles, I have need." Nayati interrupted.

"The day is good for a walk; I shall return with coke for you."

"Thank you, Brother," Yiska answered, aware that Nayati was giving them time to talk in private,"

Yahzi smiled at him in a way that touched his heart and for a moment Nayati stood there transfixed as he drank in the warmth of it. Realising suddenly that he'd held the look too long, he coloured, straightened and announced that he must go.

Yahzi giggled and Yiska grinned.

"I've ever seen Nayati embarrassed before."

"Doesn't he show his feelings?"

"He does with his family, in his own way, but with you it is different."

"Like you and Doli?"

Yiska recognised she was looking for confirmation of her developing relationship and suddenly realised how fast everything between Nayati and Yahzi had moved. She didn't really know him yet.

Yiska nodded. "It is my thinking that he likes you a lot," he answered in his best Nayati voice.

She giggled again. "I won't tell him that we spoke about this."

"It will be as you say," he said still in Nayati mode.

They fell quiet for a few minutes and Yiska guessed that she was looking for a place to start at. The silence was awkward, but he held back from breaking it, with the patience the other members of his family was accustomed to.

"I met your mother, well sort of met her. She smiled at me and said hello. I remember it because no other visitor smiled or spoke to me. There weren't many. She wasn't well, I could tell. She could barely lift the small case with your things in. They took you to the dormitory and for a while I didn't see either of you. I saw her again when she left. She was crying, and you were not with her. Even when she cried, she was a very beautiful woman."

She stopped when she witnessed a tear fall from Yiska's eye.

150

"Don't stop, tell me more about her."

"There is nothing more Yiska after she left, she didn't return."

Yiska wiped the tear away.

"Whatever I expected, whatever I hoped for, it wasn't that Yahzi. I'm amazed you still remember her."

"She was the only one apart from you that ever showed me a kindness. I wished she'd been my mother; I don't remember her. But yours was kind and caring."

"She would have liked you, she would."

"After she had gone, they moved you into the mixed race room. I was in one of three rooms that held Indians and they filled the rest with 'white' children. They operated a status system there, whites were at the top, Indians next and mixed race were at the bottom. It affected everything. Those at the bottom had all the filthy jobs, cleaning showers and toilets. The Indians tended to get cleaning jobs and some of the whites looked after the kitchen. They gave the rest of the whites positions of supervision over the Indians and the mixed races. This was a free license to bully and steal from them. They beat you more than the owners.

"I remember, when you were new to the place, they took you on jobs and you accepted a role. You didn't know any better, we didn't at that age. We did it because we didn't understand what was going on. Then after one job you must have done something wrong because you were beaten when you returned.

"I learned later that you had realised or had learned about what they were doing and refused to take part. You weren't older than five or maybe six. They left you unconscious on your bed. I had to clean your dormitory, and I thought you were dead. I told them my concerns, and the owner came to look for himself. You weren't dead, and I got a beating for being wrong. You woke up the next day.

"Your injuries took two weeks to heal, so they didn't take you on any jobs for a while. It wasn't long before they selected you for the jobs once more, but you refused again and again. When they tried to force you, you started yelling and screaming at the houses you were robbing. They beat you so many times, but you never did another robbery. They couldn't risk taking you.

"After that they left you alone. It was like you didn't exist to them. They didn't feed you; they didn't let you outside, they took all your spare clothes away and told everybody not to have anything to do with you or they would get same. Some would hit, kick or beat you for pleasure, but the beatings became fewer than before. You survived on the smallest amounts of food that some of us smuggled to you. To a few of us, David was somebody to admire.

"There's little else I can tell you. You were kind to those hurt or beaten, you cared. Few there, showed any form of kindness. They considered it a weakness that would get you a beating. When you disappeared from there, I thought you'd either escaped or you had received a beating that ended your life. It was a sad day. Until you left, there was hope."

A period of silence fell as Yahzi finished her tale and the two of them sat there unmoving lost in the painful memories of the past.

"Thank you for telling me this Yahzi, I know how painful it is but there is one thing that I find strange. Despite being beaten, as you described, somewhere along the way I learned to fight. I can defend myself in most situations, but I also can hurt people too, how did I learn this? It must have been at the orphanage."

"You have used it, already haven't you?"

"I have used it to defend myself but there was an occasion when I punched somebody unconscious with a single blow."

"There was a boy of mixed spirits, he looked more American and was big for his age. He came to the orphanage when you were about ten. You were still getting the occasional beating, and he seemed to like you. He admired your refusal to go stealing. He kept himself to himself until one day three white boys attacked him after he refused to give them his food. All three ended up unconscious in the most one-sided fight I have ever seen. It was like he danced, floated, they couldn't hit him, he only hit each boy once or twice.

"It cost him though, because the owner set eight white boys on him. He didn't want an Indian looking good against his own kind. They beat him with objects put into socks. He didn't stand a chance. He was bedridden for a long while with broken arms and ribs. You helped look after him.

"You learned to fight over a long period, how to defend yourself first and then he showed you how to hit somebody if there wasn't any other choice. He was a good teacher because I can remember two white boys attacking you for nothing. In trying to hit you somehow one broke his wrist when he hit the wall, and another fell against a bed and cracked open his head. You beat them without throwing a punch.

"When they threatened to tell the owner you told them that you would tell everybody that they had lost a fight to a mixed race boy who hadn't even hit them. They said nothing but word got around and they left you alone more and more."

"What happened to the boy who taught me to fight?"

"We heard he got shot during a robbery that went bad. It wasn't true though because he didn't do robberies. The owner had a rifle... but I have no proof."

"What was his name?"

"I don't remember. I find it hard to remember the name of anybody from there. I've learned too close everything away."

"You remembered mine."

"You were different. I didn't need to shut out somebody who was kind to me."

"One last question. When I was about fourteen, a youth of about four years older, white and nasty, hung around with two others. He had a scar under his lower lip and had a messed up nose, broken a few times. In my dreams he scares me, and this is after learning to fight. He and his gang are the ones who beat me and left me in the desert to die. I didn't fight them."

"The one you mean had a nickname, I'm sure of it, but I can't remember the name. You aren't going after him are you Yiska because if you are, think again. If we're talking about the same person, then this boy was the owner's fixer. There were several during my stay there. He's a murderer Yiska. Leave it alone."

"Relax Yahzi I'm not going after him."

"Everything I've told you; it's not made you feel any better of yourself has it?"

"No!"

"I understand how you feel Yiska, but nobody there ever tried as hard as you to break the evil cycle we were all caught in, please understand that and accept it. It doesn't count for nothing."

The gate opened and Nayati appeared. He passed each of them a bottle of coke, before opening one himself, and grinned.

"Am I supposed to accept that you walked there and back without opening a bottle?" Yiska asked.

"The walk was long, I had great thirst, and I needed two of the bottles."

Yiska laughed.

Chapter 25:
Community Spirit

Preparations for the track meet started later that day. Father Andrew met them there after lunch. He'd gathered an army of volunteers to help, both with the preparations, and for the meeting itself.

The Priest assigned several boys to repainting the lines on the cut grass for the javelin, discus and shot-putt throwing areas, inside the track. Soon a flat-bed truck arrived, loaded with trestle tables and awnings for the refreshment area, and Father Andrew asked Yiska, Nayati and Yahzi to set these up at the side of the spectator stands.

He delegated the younger members of the Muirfield team to suspending miles of bunting that would encircle both the track and the perimeter of the field; they threw themselves into the task with enthusiasm and laughter.

A group of children from the local school, complete with their teacher, unrolled a series of white bedsheets, and started to paint large, blue letters to mark the entrance and other signs. Three large, painted boxes, placed in front of the stand, offered a makeshift medal podium and a group of electrical tradesmen appeared to set up a sound system that Father Andrew would operate himself.

The work continued on all afternoon, before Father Andrew announced that marking out a parking area was the final task. Some volunteers had already drifted away homewards after a hard morning's work, but those that remained made their way to the end of the field, away from the sports track. They tied more lengths of bunting to sturdy wooden poles hammered into the hard ground, to show a track leading from this area back to the entrance. It was hard work, but the group of boys took turns, vying to knock them in with the fewest number of strikes.

The Priest then showed the boys how to use a long rope as a guideline, against which to paint a line, marking parking spaces across the width of the field. Yiska realised just how large an event this would be.

"Is there anything else to do?" he asked Father Andrew shook his head, telling him that everything had to wait until the following morning; the day of the meet itself. Father Andrew gathered up the tools they'd been using and carried them back over to the stands where he'd parked his car. Conversing with a schoolteacher, the man indicated an area behind the stands, and they made their way in that direction.

As the final volunteers slipped away, Yiska marvelled at the transformation that had taken place in the field. They'd accomplished a lot in a short time. As he looked around, the great eagle in the sky screeched out its loud and eerie call. Yiska looked up and noticed it was flying lower than its usual trajectory.

Nayati appeared at his side with Yahzi by him.

"Another warning, Brother. All is not well!" he stated, scanning the area.

"It would seem that we have visitors," Yiska told him, pointing to the far side of the track. "The group who attacked me here before."

Yahzi commented that she'd seen the group before, they often tormented the more vulnerable, homeless people, if they found them alone. One or two had received injuries by objects, thrown at them by this group.

As they watched, the leader drew a knife and cut some of the bunting affixed to the stakes, laughing as it fluttered to the ground. Yiska and Nayati told Yahzi to fetch Father Andrew and, as soon as she turned away, they both started walking towards the group of intruders.

As they approached, the group closed ranks, sneering at them.

"You didn't learn from your mistake," Yiska spoke calmly.

"If it isn't Injun boy! I told yah, our business ain't finished. New friend then?" the leader taunted.

Yiska remained calm. "What do you want here?" he asked.

"Just want payback fun," the answer came back.

"If you destroy things, there'll be nothing to have fun with," Yiska told him.

"Destroying is the fun, Injun boy!" the youth laughed.

"I cannot allow you to destroy the work that others have done," Yiska told him.

"How yah gonna stop me, Injun boy?"

Father Andrew came running up, with Yahzi behind him. "What's the problem here?" he asked noticing the cut bunting. "You again! I suggest you leave before I call the police."

"The problem appears to be me," Yiska told him. "They're back because of before."

"That's right, Injun boy, it's payback time!" the leader sneered.

"Let's end this once and for all," Yiska suggested.

"What is it you want?"

"It's time to dance. Just you and me!" the youth said.

Nayati looked at Yahzi confused. "He wants to dance?" he queried.

"He means fight," she explained.

"Nobody will fight! Leave now before I have you arrested," said Father Andrew quickly.

"So, you want to fight! If I win, do I have your word that you will leave and not return?" Yiska asked.

"If he loses against you, he won't be leading us no more," one said, laughing; his confidence in his leader clear.

"So be it then," Yiska said.

"Yiska don't do this," pleaded Father Andrew. "It will make you as bad as him."

"There's no alternative, Father Andrew. Trust me, I will not lose!" responded Yiska with a quiet confidence and winked at Father Andrew.

Mrs Willoughby approached with several members of the track team who immediately came and stood next to Yiska. Yiska asked them to move back. Mrs Willoughby guessed what was about to happen and raised her hand to her mouth in horror.

"Please form a circle and sit down," Yiska asked them and they followed his request, leaving just him and his opponent standing in the ring. "I am ready," he stated.

The leader grinned in anticipation, raised his fists and started to approach Yiska. Yiska watched him, adopting a loose, open stance, but kept his hands by his side. The two circled, Yiska waiting, the other looking for an opening.

The gang started to shout encouragement to their leader, goading him to strike out, and it was he who threw the first punch, towards Yiska's head. Yiska saw it coming, stepped to one side, and the punch whistled by. There was laughter at this and Yiska sensed the anger building up inside the youth. Again the youth shot his fist out, aiming for the same target and once more Yiska stepped aside.

The youth changed tactics, put his head down and charged at him. Once again Yiska moved to the side, but this time he used his hands to push the youth on his way as he passed. He sprawled to the ground, much to the amusement of his gang. He got up instantly and repeated the charge, instantly regretting it as he lurched to the ground once more. The rage in his eyes, as he stood, was clear to all the onlookers. He drew the knife he'd used on the bunting from his pocket, opened the blade and held it in front of him as he approached Yiska again.

Mrs Willoughby screamed and made to get up, but Nayati, seated next to her, held her firm.

"Trust my brother; he knows what he is doing," he told her, but she couldn't watch and turned her face away.

As the boy moved closer to Yiska, he waved the knife back and forth in front of him, and suddenly lunged. Yiska, waiting for this, turned sideways and pulled at the arm with the knife, forcing the boy off-balance once more. He fell to the floor in a crumpled heap.

Yiska stepped on his arm and pulled the knife from his hand. He passed it to Nayati before releasing the boy's arm. Yiska's attacker stood once more, his rage overflowing completely, robbing him of any rational thought, and launched himself at Yiska.

This time Yiska moved backwards, and the boy fell flat in front of him. Yiska bent down and twisted the youth's hand behind his back and gripped it tight.

"Are we finished?" he asked, in the same calm voice.

The gang members rose from their seated position and spat on the ground in front of their leader's prone position. Then they walked away in disappointment and disgust.

Yiska released the boy's arm and took a step backwards, allowing him room to get up. The youth raised himself; the anger having dissipated while he was down. He kept his head low, not meeting Yiska's eyes and said, "It's finished."

He and walked away.

Father Andrew stood and confronted Yiska. "That could have ended differently; especially when he drew his knife," he said.

Yiska nodded his agreement. "It seemed the right way to deal with this character," he answered.

Mrs Willoughby prevented further discussion when she hugged Yiska tight and told him how brave he was and how proud she was of him for not partaking in this act of violence. He hugged her back.

Nayati came forward and teased, "You move almost as fast as your brother!"

Yiska grinned at him and then moved with the speed of a cat to slap his brother on the shoulder. But Nayati caught his hand before it made contact.

"It is as I say. You move almost at the speed of your brother." They both laughed.

Yahzi stepped forward. "Yiska, this is what you were like at the orphanage at the end when they punished you. Sometimes they were too big, and too many for you to win," she told him. He thanked her for the information, pleased with what he learned.

They repaired the cut bunting and made their way back into town. Yiska suggested to Father Andrew that it would be a good idea to ask Father Michael to bring his team a little earlier so that the two teams would get some time to socialise with their adversaries before battle so to speak.

He explained the competitive nature that he and Nayati shared with each other, saying that competition was more special because they understood each other so well. If the two teams shared what they did, then the competition would be more intense. Father Andrew liked this and would relish a little extra time with his friend Father Michael.

Nayati and Yiska were also looking forward to seeing him.

At the soup kitchen, the well-established routine, continued with its normal comfortable atmosphere. Nayati and Yahzi were serving, whilst Father Andrew and Yiska talked to their guests.

Silence fell when a black and white sedan drove up, stopping just short of them. A police deputy emerged from the vehicle and made his way to the van. One or two of the homeless disappeared into the shadows.

Nayati watched him walking towards them before recognising the man who had taken him to the sheriff's office. The deputy removed his hat and scratched his head.

"You're working late, Nayati."

"As are you, Deputy!" responded Nayati.

"I don't suppose you have any of that broth going spare, have you?" he asked.

Nayati ladled some into a bowl and gave it to the deputy.

"Thanks," he said. "I've not eaten since breakfast and it's been a mighty long day of paperwork!" He accepted the hunk of bread that Yahzi passed to him. "It's good that you're no longer on the streets, Yahzi."

She nodded. "I am with Nayati now," she told him.

"Well, it's Nayati I've come to visit, if you can let me have him for a few minutes," he said.

Nayati emerged silently from the van and stood in front of the deputy. "There is something you need?" he enquired.

"No, I've come to apologise for the misunderstanding the other day. I was… Well, I was a little heavy-handed; the way I treated you. I'm sorry for that. You're doing a good thing here, and that needs encouraging. I wish others could follow your example," he said.

Nayati kept the surprise from his face. "It is a good job that you do also," he told the deputy holding out his hand in the western fashion for him to shake.

The deputy moved away to Father Andrew and sat down beside him, nodding to the street people as he passed.

"I have come to offer my services, Father. I have spare time in the evenings and wondered if you need some help at the youth club. The club keeps a lot of youngsters out of trouble and it would do no harm to improve relationships between the police department and the young people of this town."

"There's always work that needs good people to help, Deputy," Father Andrew told him. "The children would gain from that. It would be most beneficial for them to have an upstanding member of the community spend time with them. It would make them feel like people care. Sometimes they just need somebody to talk to, somebody to listen to their problems. You could have a massive impact on their lives and help to keep them on track. Why don't you drop by tomorrow and let me show you the ropes?"

Chapter 26:
The Track Meet

Yiska, Nayati and Yahzi arrived at the trackside early the next morning. Father Andrew had arranged for the delivery of refreshments straight to the track and he needed them to assist with the unloading of them. Mrs Willoughby and Mrs Baker would arrive shortly afterwards to arrange and display the refreshment area.

The meet was due to start at ten o'clock, so that the athletes could avoid running during the worst of the mid-afternoon heat. By then only field events would take place with relays set late to close the event. The competitors started to arrive just after eight, and Yiska was looking forward to introducing them to the team from Mason. Father Andrew tested out the public announcement system, and the volume of his voice booming across the field surprised Nayati.

"His voice will reach to the spirit world," he told Yiska, who laughed at the surprise in his brother's tone.

Just as he finished speaking, an old, yellow school bus drove through the entrance, the driver blasting his horn in greeting. Yiska spotted Father Michael at the steering wheel and waved enthusiastically, a large grin of delight forming. The bus parked at the bottom of the field and the occupants started to pour out.

Father Michael led them towards an area at the side of the track where two open-sided tents would house the teams. Inside, benches were already set out for the athletes. Nayati pointed the team towards them as they approached and suggested that they unload their bags.

Yiska moved to Father Michael and shook his hand warmly. "It's good to see you Father Michael, how are you?" he asked, smiling his pleasure.

"Happy to see you too, Yiska! I can't wait to learn what's been happening; Father Andrew's only told me snippets, to make sure I stop over tonight; so I've had to organise another driver for later!"

"There's plenty to share, that's for sure!" Yiska told him. "The rest of the Muirfield athletes will be here soon and we'll introduce them to your team and let them get to know each other a bit before they warm up. Competition against friends is better that competition against rivals."

"I like the thinking behind that, Yiska," replied Father Michael.

Just as he finished, Nayati came over with members of the Muirfield team. As the introductions between the teenagers were being made, Nayati greeted Father Michael and introduced Yahzi before the Priest sought his friend and colleague who was still making adjustments to the sound system. They returned soon after with a request for Nayati and Yiska.

"It would seem that Mason is short of a distance runner Yiska, and I would ask that you represent us," Father Michael asked.

"I would, but are you sure that you wouldn't prefer Nayati to run for you?"

"I'm afraid that we are short-handed too in the field events and need somebody for the javelin. Father Michael tells me that you sometimes fish with a spear Nayati, so you are probably adept at throwing it." Father Andrew interrupted.

"It is a wise choice you have made for the spear, for my brother is still learning the skill after many years of trying." Nayati said and grinned at his Brother. "It will be as you ask Father Andrew."

"Thank you both."

A few spectators started to arrive next, coming early to secure the best seats, and it wasn't long before a steady stream started to pour in. Some made themselves comfortable on grassy areas whilst others filled the seats. Several busses of supporters from Mason also arrived and despite the competitive nature of the day the atmosphere remained relaxed and gentle.

Father Andrew welcomed everybody on the PA and announced the order of events for the day for those who had not bought a program. Track athletes emerged from their tents for the first event and the crowd cheered at the sound of the gun that sent them sprinting down the track.

Yahzi left Nayati's side to help Mrs Willoughby and Mrs Baker at the refreshments area where two queues had grown, one for drinks and one for food. She was soon hard at work selling drinks alongside Mrs Baker where the demand seemed endless.

A sour looking, tall, thin man, in his thirties sneered at her while he waited his turn and started to complain loudly about the time he had to wait in the queue before being served. His aggression fuelled one or two others who also voiced their disapproval and before long the hostility grew too much for Mrs Baker who suggested that some of the complainers should volunteer their time to help instead of moaning.

Someone from the queue called her something rude, and she invited the unknown person to come and say it to her face. Yahzi calmed her down, telling her to ignore the comments and for a moment she took her advice but then the man who had started all the fuss reached the counter and faced Yahzi.

"Give me two cokes squaw," he snarled.

Yahzi ignored the racial content and placed two bottles of coke in front of him.

"What's this squaw? I said two bottles of lemonade."

Again, Yahzi ignored the racial aspect and, keeping calm, apologised for the misunderstanding. She took the cokes back and replaced them with lemonade.

"Are you stupid or something squaw I asked for two cokes and these aint cokes?"

"Since you seem to have a problem making your mind up which drink you want sir, I suggest you move aside and let me serve somebody who knows exactly what they want." Yahzi said, giving the man her most winning smile.

"Why you low down stinking little Indian squaw, how dare you talk to me like that."

He leant forward aggressively with menace in his eyes flashing like the last rays at sunset, and Yahzi thought he would attack her. She took a step backwards.

"I've had enough from you. You want a drink so badly take mine." Mrs Baker suddenly intervened, throwing a cup of water directly into the man's face. The man stood upright and took a step backwards at the shock of the cold water.

"Why you old..."

He never got to finish his sentence for another voice interrupted.

"You need to come with me sir, you can explain why you are so intent on causing trouble to the Sherriff. Anybody else have a complaint about the service here?" Nobody replied.

"Thank you, Deputy Williams, your arrival is most welcome."

"Glad to be of service Mrs Baker, I saw everything that happened. Be careful not to slip like that again though won't you, I wouldn't want to see you get hurt," he said, giving the old woman a wink."

"Thank you, Deputy, I'll take extra care."

"Good to see you Yahzi, well done for keeping so calm."

Yahzi blushed slightly but smiled at the deputy before he led the troublemaker away.

On the track Yiska had taken up a position for the longest race of the day, the five-thousand metres; twelve and a half laps of the track. At first, he thought he was running the same race he'd competed in during his time in Mason, but delight spread across his face to be taking on a much longer distance.

Nayati, who had been helping Yiska form bonds between the opposing athletes, fetched Yahzi so that she could watch.

"When you win do not make the others seem bad brother," Nayati called out.

"I will leave it until the last lap," Yiska replied grinning.

"By the time we get to the last lap Yiska you will be too far behind to catch us," one of the other competitors called out and a few others echoed his sentiments.

Yiska grinned again.

"They make the mistake of challenging Yiska. They will lose." Nayati told Yahzi.

Father Michael started the race and at the gun the athletes raced the first hundred metres jostling for position.

Yiska started off sedately and let them move away from him while he settled in last place.

"He has not started well Nayati," Yahzi stated with a concerned frown.

"There are many journeys around the track. Yiska knows this," Nayati responded.

By the end of the fourth lap the athletes had established a consistent pace and stretched out in a line spanning thirty metres. Yiska remained at the rear and closed the gap behind the boy in front.

There were nine athletes in front of him and eight and a half laps to go. Forming a strategy to overtake one per lap and the last in the final half lap, there was no doubt in his mind about winning this. He wanted to win but Nayati had been right about not making it appear easy, there was no need to attract attention, but he did have to win. The competitive nature of distance running was a challenge he really enjoyed; as much about competing with yourself as it was against others. Putting his plan into action, he overtook his first competitor on the straight, in front of the seated area.

"Yiska has made his move," Nayati told Yahzi who smiled but couldn't help thinking that he was too far back in the field.

Yiska overtook two more in the same place on subsequent laps and Nayati realised what his brother was doing. He told Yahzi.

"How do you know this," she asked.

"He is my brother, and we have raced many times. Yiska will win the race easily but does not wish to show how fast he really is."

"Why?"

"The others in the race would feel bad for they would lose by a great distance."

"He cares about the others?"

"They are as friends."

Yiska overtook the others until there was just one in front of him and half a lap to go. He increased his pace to a sprint and finished the race thirty metres ahead of the second place athlete. The crowd cheered at his sprint and he grinned as he passed the finish line. He turned and greeted his competitors with a handshake. Fathers Andrew and Michael came over to congratulate him and both noticed that he was hardly short of breath.

"You could have won that easily Yiska," Father Michael said.

"They gave me a good run Father," Yiska told them, leaving to find his brother.

Yahzi head back to the refreshment stall leaving them alone for a while.

"There is time before I throw the spear."

"Is there something you want to do?"

"I am in need of food."

"Wouldn't be fries appealing to you by any chance."

"You are correct."

"The diner?"

"Yes."

They slipped away returning an hour later. The track events had just culminated with the shorter sprint events and there was an interlude for the spectators to picnic before the field events started. The boys sought Yahzi before heading off to the javelin arena.

"You must have a practise Nayati, these are not exactly like the fishing spears," Yiska told him.

"It is a spear and I will throw without difficulty."

Nayati watched as some of his competitors tried out their practise runs. One called Nayati over.

"I heard you're throwing against us, I hope you are not as good as your brother is at running," he said good naturedly. "I'm Ben."

The young man threw the javelin and Nayati congratulated his effort after it landed a good distance away.

Nayati selected a javelin from the rack and felt the weight of it. He positioned it above his shoulder and scribed the throwing motion without releasing it.

"It is not heavy in my hand; it was my thinking that it would weigh more."

"You have thrown one of these before, haven't you?"

"I have not."

"Watch my run up and my technique for launching it and we'll see if we can save you some embarrassment. It is not as easy as it looks."

169

"It will be as you say."

Ben threw a second, launching it into the distance.

"Can you throw it further? It's a practise throw, to improve technique."

"I will make a throw now."

Nayati took a longer run up and launched the javelin effortlessly. It sailed past Ben's effort "Are you sure you have never thrown a javelin before?"

"I have used spears for fishing but not for throwing."

"Can you throw it further?"

Nayati grinned. "Wait for the competition."

Ben grinned back recognising the challenge.

"Just remember, don't step over the line. If you do your throw won't count," he said sportingly.

Nayati moved back to his Brother and Yahzi.

"How far exactly can you throw it?" Yiska asked.

"I did not throw it far."

"I will win by just enough as you showed earlier."

Nayati won the Javelin by a few metres and Ben was the first to congratulate him; the other field events finished shortly after.

The track meet was a huge success, the large crowd that watched were supportive to all the athletes, and the two teams competed with a sporting spirit. Mason won the overall event by just two points; their first win in four years, and Father Michael savoured the moment.

The two teams mingled after the competition had finished, as they had all day, with new friendships forged and old ones rekindled. They all helped take down the bunting and the temporary structures, before forming an army that worked like locusts to rid the field of the litter left by the hordes of visitors. Father Andrew and Father Michael pronounced the meet as the best and organised the clear-up operations with smiles on their faces.

Chapter 27:
Dinner

Despite volunteering her services all day, dinner that evening was at Mrs Willoughby's, at her specific invitation. Determined to enjoy this whirl of social activity, she had invited the two Priests as well as Nayati, Yiska and Yahzi to eat with her. She hurried home, straight after the competition finished, to prepare lasagne, which had become Nayati's favourite dish. Her soft spot, for all the young people that had entered her life recently, was running at full throttle; Her maternal instincts in full flow.

The success of the day overjoyed Father Michael and Father Andrew, and they too were in fine spirits. Whilst dinner cooked Father Michael told Mrs Willoughby of the work that Nayati and Yiska had done to save the youth club from being condemned. She told both Priests what good boys they were, although they already knew this, and how they'd improved her quality of life.

Father Andrew then told Father Michael what had happened since the boy's arrival. There was laughter again at Nayati's misunderstanding of the word address, and more so when he opened his hands and imitating wide-eyed innocence. He also related the success of the soup kitchen, and how Yahzi had been the first of the homeless people to leave the streets and return to society, and how proud he was of her and the role the others had played in her transition.

Father Michael said that he wanted to start a soup kitchen for the homeless too but finding volunteer help had been difficult. He'd arranged for several restaurants to pass him their left-over food and even found two women able to collect and prepare it but as yet he'd no van to operate from and no volunteers to man the kitchen.

Mrs Willoughby was the perfect hostess and positively enjoyed being run off her feet, ensuring that her guests were comfortable and content. It wasn't until, after they had eaten, that Nayati insisted that she stopped and joined them that she finally took off her apron and sat down with a cup of her favourite tea.

Father Andrew asked Yahzi what her plans were, and she explained that Mrs Willoughby was helping her get a job. She told them that she didn't really mind what she did as long as people treated her decently.

"If she works as hard as she did today then she will be an asset to anyone. Oh, and did you learn what happened to her and Mrs Baker today?"

When nobody answered in the affirmative, she told the story about the man who was racially unpleasant and bent on causing trouble. She complimented Yahzi on the way she had been so calm and restrained and praised Mrs Baker for throwing the water at the horrible man.

"I'm not sure we should praise that; it might have escalated the problem." Father Andrew stated.

"If nothing else it was brave of her," Mrs Willoughby said supporting her friend.

Yahzi continued the story, telling of how Deputy Williams had arrested the man and warning Mrs Baker to be careful not to slip again. They all laughed at this and Nayati promised to thank the man later at the youth club.

Nayati asked Yahzi why she hadn't told him about all this earlier and she told him honestly that she wasn't sure how he would react.

"It is my thinking that I would say his way with people needed to change."

"How do you think he would respond?"

"I am thinking that he would have said sorry."

Everybody in the room laughed.

"It would seem that I am wrong in my thinking."

They laughed again.

"People like that don't apologise Nayati, he most likely would have hit you. He was a bully, a sexist and a racist. All problems that stem from not understanding differences between people and resenting what they don't understand," Father Michael explained.

"Niyol says that differences between people are good because we can learn from them. There are a lot of differences between Nayati and I and we are stronger together because of it."

"Niyol is a very knowledgeable man by the sounds of it," Father Andrew said profoundly.

"My grandfather has lived many years, there is little he does not know," Nayati said proudly.

"What did you think about the verbal assault from that man Yahzi?" Mrs Willoughby asked.

"I've experienced this before. At the orphanage they separated us by our colour and those who weren't white got treated poorly. When I was on the streets people that passed me were often unkind, rude and even physical sometimes, colour didn't really seem to make much difference then, more the fact that I was homeless. Today I am clean, have somewhere to stay and still somebody is horrible to me.

Nothing seems to change this. I choose to walk away because I don't want to be like them. Here, we have white people, an Indian and two of mixed spirits. I use this term because it is how Nayati describes himself and it is better than the names used on the streets. Everyone here respects each other and there is no racism, sexism or any other ism. I wish to be with people like this."

"Well said Yahzi," Father Michael responded.

"This is what Father Andrew and I want to achieve with the young people at our youth and athletics club. Our efforts are working. In some ways we are too late to change many of the older peoples thinking, it's too ingrained in their ways but with the young we have a chance. The homeless too, they all have something in common despite their native origins. Even here it's a struggle, some have an aversion to society, let alone anything else," the Priest said.

"All we can do is keep trying and keep praying." Mrs Willoughby added.

The evening passed too quickly and as the two Priests said their goodnights, Yiska asked if the two of them could spare some time before Father Michael returned to Mason. They found some time for him after the kitchen run, even though it was late, but Yiska didn't seem to mind. Mrs Willoughby started to busy herself clearing up and humming a tune happily before encouraging Nayati and Yahzi to go out back and get some fresh air on the porch seat. They needed no more encouragement to seek time alone.

Chapter 28:
As One

"It has been a good day Nayati!" Yahzi almost whispered as she nestled against him.

"We've made friends and have new stories to tell which will stay with us. Like you winning the Javelin and Yiska the distance race."

"This and more."

"You mean like the horrible man at the refreshment stall."

"That and more. Grandfather told me, I would meet people who do not like Indians or those of mixed spirits. I listened well but there are more than I believed."

"There are. Yiska and I both lived a nightmare because of who and what we are. These people never want to know us."

"Grandfather says they fear what they do not know and understand."

"But we are people just like them."

"Not like them, for we think in different ways."

"We are human beings Nayati."

"I understand what you say. The body is the same, different colours sometimes, but we think what we learn from our teachers. I learn from a wise old man, I learn from my sister, my brother, the Priests, Mrs Willoughby and Yahzi. All are good; they care and help others. It is my thinking it is wise to choose people like these to learn from."

"The man today, who taught him?"

"I have no knowledge, but it is one who believes as he does."

"It's horrible Nayati, I don't want to live in a place where there is hatred and bad feeling."

The past is the past. You are free to leave. It is my thinking you could have left long ago when you escaped from that place. But you remain, why is this so?"

"I didn't know anybody; I didn't know where to go and I used to believe wherever I went I would meet more people like the ones who hurt me and kept me prisoner. I had more food from the soup kitchen in a few months than I had received in a year at the orphanage. Living on the streets had a few problems but once I moved to the cemetery, everyone left me alone. There was a peace there I couldn't get anywhere else."

"Did you talk to the spirits there, or the God the white people speak to?"

"No."

"I learn most people talk to spirits or God."

"For me it would be the spirits Nayati. I am Navajo. I don't know anyone who passed into the spirit world."

"Your family?"

"I know nothing about my past, before the orphanage. I don't remember who took me there. I don't remember a mother or a father. Yiska now knows more about his past than I do."

"Is this a matter you would seek to change as my Brother does?"

"No. I am Yahzi and I am Navajo. My family are people who care for me."

"This is a good way. If Yiska thinks only this, we would be in the forest."

"If you weren't here, then you wouldn't have met me."

"This is true, perhaps I am glad Yiska feels other than you."

Yahzi gave him her best smile and lost herself in the blue of his eyes. Nayati held the look and smiled back melting her heart and encouraging her eyes to moisten.

Mrs Willoughby opened her back door and saw the two of them snuggled close on the seat and smiled.

"Sorry to disturb you two but I've come to tell you it's time to go to the soup kitchen. I know what it's like when you talk, the time seems to pass faster."

"Thank you Mrs Willoughby I didn't realise it was late already," Yahzi told her.

The two of them left after saying goodnight and walked at a sedate pace not wishing their time alone to end a moment before it had to.

"Nayati, I would like it if we held hands as we walk."

"My Brother does this when he is alone with Doli. It was my thinking it is against the Navajo ways."

"And now?"

"I would try this. It pleases my sister and Yiska to do this. It may please me also."

"And me."

Yahzi took his hand and interlocked their fingers. She squeezed it gently. It feels good, yes?"

"It is as you say."

Yiska was already at the kitchen when they got there, and he noticed their joined hands. He had a brief notion, suggesting an opportunity to tease Nayati about this as he remembered the hard time Nayati had given him when he first held Doli's hand. He decided against it as he recognised the happiness exuding form both of them. His thoughts focussed in on Doli and how much he missed her, and he hastened to greet them to thwart the memories dominating his mind.

"Can you two operate the serving duties tonight?"

"What are you doing Yiska," Yahzi asked.

"I want to speak to Father Andrew and Father Michael before Father Michael returns to Mason."

"It will be as you ask Brother."

"I will see you back at Mrs Willoughby's then."

Yiska thanked them and went to find the two Priests.

Father Andrew came over to them five minutes later.

"Will you two be all right? Father Michael and I need to go."

"We can take care of everything Father," Yahzi told him.

He disappeared, and they started to serve the first of the evening's customers.

Deputy Williams dropped by and told them he'd charged the man he'd removed from the refreshment stall earlier, a minor offence that would see a fine imposed for his behaviour. He congratulated her for her restraint, promising he would do everything in his power to stop blatant displays of racism happening, and to punish those who continued to partake in it. Yahzi thanked him and told him she was pleased he passed by when he did. She poured him a bowl of soup and Nayati made him a coffee.

They noticed how the homeless didn't disappear when the deputy showed up now like they did when he first had. Others were trying to change attitudes too.

When the kitchen closed for the night Nayati locked everything up and he and Yahzi started to walk back to Mrs Willoughby's.

"You would like to hold hands?" Nayati asked.

Yahzi answered by placing her hand in his.

"There is a matter I wish to talk to you about." Nayati stated.

"Talk away Nayati."

"When my Brother's journey ends, I hope to return to my home. A good day and a sad day. I will say goodbye to friends here. I do not wish to say goodbye to you. It is my thinking we are becoming as one and I would like it if you come with me.

"My home is peaceful and beautiful. My sister and grandfather are good people and will welcome you. In the mountains, life is different and hard in winter, but you are Navajo and would live as the Navajo. There are no people who act badly."

Yahzi looked at him in an adoring way, and a single tear rolled down her cheek.

"Sounds perfect; I want to be with you. I will work hard to become worthy of you, Nayati." She reached up and kissed him on the cheek. "I will come with you," she said and leaned into his arms.

"This is a good thing. It is so we celebrate good things here, we should do this with Yiska and Mrs Willoughby."

"What do you have in mind?"

"My Brother and Doli like to take food on a short journey and eat at a place they like."

"You mean a picnic."

"This is the word he uses."

"It's a great idea, Mrs Willoughby would love it."

"It will be so."

Chapter 29:
Shame

Father Andrew took Yiska and Father Michael back to his home and set about making them coffee. He placed a mug in front of each of them and sat down beside them.

"I can tell something is bothering you Yiska. You are far too quiet, and you haven't smiled all evening despite having had a great day," Father Michael said.

"You know whatever you tell us is in the strictest confidence so spill it and let's see if we can't make you smile again." Father Andrew added.

"What I tell you is in confidence because my brother doesn't know yet. Telling him will be hard."

"I thought there weren't any secrets between the two of you," Father Andrew queried.

"There isn't. But I've just discovered things from my past, things I don't like about myself. I am ashamed of what I did."

"The things that happened at the orphanage were beyond your control Yiska, you were a child. Unless the spirits return your memories, you can't possibly know much about what happened," Father Michael argued.

"I know because Yahzi told me some of what she remembered. Father Andrew was there."

Father Andrew related the details of what Yahzi remembered and shocked his colleague at the amount of violence committed at the orphanage and the amount Yiska had endured.

"Let me get this right Yiska, from about the age of six you refused to take part in any of the wrong doings going on, despite the punishments they dished out to you."

"Yes!"

"I'm amazed, first because of your sense of right and wrong at such a young age and second, you survived against all the odds."

"I have no memories or any certainty I'll get them. What Yahzi remembers is enough for now."

"Forgive me Yiska but I am not understanding what your problem is with all this." Father Michael stated.

"To understand, this happened after I left the orphanage."

Yiska told them both how, almost beaten to death, Niyol found him in the desert by chance. He told them of the old man who cared for him, who trained him, gave him an identity and the gift of a family. He told them about Doli and how much he loved her and then explained what sort of characters they both are.

"At the orphanage I was nobody, I had no personality, no family and no one to care for. Nobody cared for me either. I had no identity. Niyol gave me a culture and, someone to live up to. He gave me his family, Nayati and Doli. He gave me a life so good, I can never repay him for it. I try every day to be worthy of him and everything he has given me, and I try every day to be worthy of the love my family gives me and now I find out I did awful things, things I am ashamed of. I cannot go back knowing I am not who they think I am."

Yiska stopped talking, and a silence hung in the room. Father Michael refilled the coffee mugs and Yiska sipped at his, unable to look at them.

"There are several ways to view this Yiska. First, you did as ordered, it was how to survive; you were not to blame.

Second, you stopped doing what was wrong when you understood it was wrong despite the punishment you took. You chose right at the point of understanding. Third, what happened so long ago bears no correlation to the person sitting next to me right now. You are not that child now. Fourth, you have more than paid for the crimes you committed through being beaten, starved and eventually left for dead. You've nothing to atone for." Father Michael said.

"I concur," Father Andrew added.

"Why do I feel like this? Yahzi spent three years punishing herself for her own part in the thefts. One for each year of her involvement. She needed punishment for what she did."

"If she had come to us and spoke about this, we would have told her what we are telling you."

"But she is better for doing it, she has placed her past behind her and is moving on?"

"Atonement is always good for the soul and can lead to absolution," Father Andrew muttered.

"Then I want to atone, find absolution, because this is eating me up inside."

"So this is the help you want from us Yiska. It goes against the grain to make somebody atone for something they had no choice in. You are innocent," Father Michael said, with an air of defeat.

"I know you well enough so I will suggest something. You can decide if it is worthy." Father Andrew stated. "It has been a plan of mine to start a soup kitchen in Mason and run it as father Michael does here. I know about the work you've been doing here and the success you are having. So here is my proposal. You will run the soup kitchen for the period of one year and help at the youth club and at the athletics track. All these worthy causes and one year because it's how long you were partaking in the robberies. You can use a room at the back of the church. After one year you are to return home to your family and not one day later. Are we agreed?"

"Yes, in part."

"Why only part?"

"What you are suggesting is just work, I need challenge and difficulty."

"I will consider this for a time."

"Thank you."

"There is one more thing Yiska." Father Michael added. "At the end of the year you understand you'll receive your absolution; your sins will be forgiven. It is important you forgive yourself. Can you do this?"

"I think so."

"It's late now, go back to Mrs Willoughby's."

"It will not be easy telling your Brother Yiska." Father Andrew added as an afterthought."

"I know, but he'll understand."

Yiska thanked the two Priests and slipped out leaving them to ponder more on what had happened.

The next two weeks passed by quickly. They became more involved with the youth club before going to the soup kitchen. But it was at the soup kitchen where they made a real difference to the street people visiting it every night.

Nayati and Yahzi were trying to persuade another young woman to leave the streets and start a fresh life. They had spoken to Mrs Willoughby who had approached her neighbour, Mrs Baker, to offer the girl lodgings, and she had agreed. Father Andrew found her a part-time job in a fabric shop, run by an old friend of his; a friend who would do everything to help the girl. Nayati and Yahzi had taken Serena to Mrs Baker, who wasted no time in getting her cleaned up. They had taken her to the fabric shop on her first day and collected her after her shift. She had made a good impression on the owner, and everything looked bright for her future. She joined the vigil at the soup kitchen and received the same reception from the street people as Yahzi had.

The success didn't stop there, though. Father Andrew and Yiska had been persuading two middle-aged members of the homeless community to come off the streets.

The two were friends and Father Andrew had found them work on a local farm and an old house they could rent together. They also returned to the soup kitchen to help and there were now more volunteers than needed. Each member reached out, forming new relationships and offering advice and support.

Chapter 30:
The Letter

The postman delivered a large envelope to Mrs Willoughby's house the next day. She opened it and took out a sheaf of paper that she had been waiting for. Her hands shook a little as she read through the contents. Tears flowed down her face as she returned the sheets to the envelope. She replaced her slippers with shoes and placed the envelope in her bag, before stepping out and making her way to the church. Father Andrew was there with a broom in his hand, sweeping between the pews.

"Afternoon, Mrs Willoughby," he said smiling, but then stopped work as he noticed the misery on her face.

"What is it my dear?" he asked gently.

She gave him the envelope which he took, opened and read the contents.

"That poor boy! Hasn't he been through enough?" he exclaimed. "We must tell him, and soon. Good news or bad, he's waited so long for this information. I'll tell him tonight, before we go to the soup kitchen. If the news affects him badly, the work might ease his mind for a while."

"Come over to my house tonight; I'll need to know that he is all right," Mrs Willoughby demanded.

The Priest sought Yiska to tell him about the letter and found him with Nayati and Yahzi at the youth club where they were making repairs to the counter area. The wooden panels forming the sides of the counter were coming apart where the glue that held them to the frames had loosened with age. Splintered and sharp, they needed replacing. Deputy Williams, who gave his free time in the evenings, had brought in some new panels and wood glue for them to make the repairs.

Father Andrew walked in and greeted them. Taking Yiska to one side, he told him he'd received information about his parents. Yiska agreed to the proposed meeting time and returned to finish the work he had started.

After Father Andrew had left, Yiska told Nayati and Yahzi what they'd said. Pleased for his brother, Nayati spoke up. "You've waited a long time for this," he told him.

Yiska nodded but did not return the smile; a sense of foreboding consumed him. Now the moment of truth was imminent, the information they'd found worried him. Nayati noticed the lack of enthusiasm and could only guess at the reasons behind this. Yahzi hugged Yiska in a show of support and encouragement.

"Any news is better than none," she told him, "because it's easier to deal with what you know, than what you only imagine."

He nodded a grateful response and turned back to his work.

Later that evening they gathered at Mrs Willoughby's, awaiting Father Andrew's arrival. Nayati asked Yiska if he'd prefer to hear the news alone, but he told his brother that there were no secrets between them.

"If I cannot share with my family, then who could I share with?" he asked Nayati.

Father Andrew arrived a little later than he'd expected, which added to the growing anticipation that the others felt.

Already knowing most of the information that Father Andrew was about to reveal, Mrs Willoughby kept herself busy, only appearing when Father Andrew arrived. She brought in tea and biscuits, and fussed about, trying to relieve some of the tension in the air. Father Andrew removed the folded envelope from his breast pocket and placed it on the coffee table, whilst greeting them all and thanking them for the work they had undertaken earlier at the Youth Centre.

Poor Yiska found it difficult to take his eyes off the envelope and could not follow the conversation taking place. Father Andrew noticed this and, understanding the reason, picked up the envelope and removed the sheets of paper from within.

"As you know, Mrs Willoughby and I've tried to research your family through a variety of different mediums, Yiska, but we could not find very much. Because of this, I hired a private investigator to uncover as much information as he could on your behalf," he stated.

Yiska interrupted. "This would have cost you a great deal of money, Father Andrew. I hope that you will give me the bill for this."

"There'll be no bill, young man! The work you and your brother did for Father Michael, and I has been priceless, so it's you that should give a bill to me for all the good things you've done!" He moved on to avoid hearing Yiska's response.

"In front of me is information about both of your parents. Since it's an itemised account, there are details explaining the origin of how and where the information came from, as well as what they discovered. As you cannot read this yourself, I would ask that you allow me to read the relevant parts to you."

Yiska nodded his agreement.

"Would you like to hear about your father first or your mother?" Father Andrew asked.

"My mother, please."

"Your mother, Katherine, was born in a small town in Idaho. Her parents died when she was young, both of heart disease. This explains how they met, for they were patients in the same hospital clinic. When they died, within six months of each other, and when she was ten, your mother went to live with her grandmother. Her grandmother died during your mother's eighteenth year, leaving her alone in the world with no other relative.

She started working at a war veteran's hospital and trained to be a nurse. It was here that she met your father who was recovering from a war injury. A year later she married him, and you were born two years later on November the first 1946. Your mother fell ill just before your third birthday and went into hospital for several months.

Her neighbour and friend, Freida Williams looked after you, until she returned home. Diagnosed with terminal cancer during her stay, she made it her sole task to seek somewhere for you to go when she could no longer look after you and died soon after your admittance to the Muirfield orphanage.

There was no way she could've known the dark secrets concealed behind the closed doors of that place. The neighbour is still alive and the only person the detective tracked down who knew your mother well. She's lived in Canada for the last twelve years, but her address is here."

Yiska sat without expression, while Father Andrew drank some coffee. There was little additional information here above what he already knew, but the friend that lived in Canada interested him. Perhaps Mrs Willoughby would help to contact her. He wanted to know more about his mother, the person she was, what she liked, what her talents were and a hundred other things. Pleased with this idea of tracking down her good friend, his original worries about what they might discover began to dissipate. He asked Father Andrew to tell him about his father.

"There is some basic information about your father, but this area of research is lacking. Our investigator drew a blank in his research, despite his best efforts. He found only what he could access. This is what he unearthed…

"Your father's name was Yas, which is the Navajo word for snow. There could be many reasons they called him this, but we just don't know. We've already heard that your mother helped to nurse him back to health in the military hospital before they married. It wasn't possible to discover what he did for a living before the war, or where they lived during their married life.

"There was nothing in his name–leases, bank details etc. They were all in your mother's name; all the bills were paid from your mother's account, I guess because he was overseas so much. As this line of investigation revealed nothing, the investigator tried to find out about his service career. Details for this are classified and sealed. This means that nobody can find out about what's inside until a certain number of years pass, when they'll become unsealed and available to read by all. Certain parts of your father's records were available, this is what he found:

"They drafted your father into the army to fight a war with which he didn't agree. We know this because he objected to fighting and tried to gain the status of 'conscientious objector', but they dismissed his claim and they forced him to fight abroad. He wrote letters home, telling of the awful things he saw and what he did. They never posted them; they vetted all letters before posting; the military worried about information being leaked to the enemy.

"As an infantry soldier, he would have had contact with the enemy at close quarters and, if he was a genuine pacifist, what he saw would have appalled him. He received two medals for bravery; for saving the life of injured

189

comrades. In both cases, the commendations he received from his senior officers were of the highest calibre.

"Injured, during his second act of heroism, they sent home him to convalesce. That's when he met your mother. He remained in the army's service during this time and returned to the war when he was fit and well. However, although he was physically well, nobody had assessed his mental capacity to fight again.

"In subsequent forays with the enemy, he charged, firing his weapon above the enemies' heads! Somehow, he survived these encounters, and his superiors transferred to a special unit because of his courage in the face of conflict but he was shot and killed on his first mission with the new unit. The investigator believes that he avoided shooting at the enemy, choosing to end his life rather than fight in a war in which he didn't believe; there have been many such cases documented.

"They never returned his body home, but your mother received a letter saying how he had died, and she received a widow's pension till her death. You were born six months after Yas died. It's possible he didn't even know his wife was pregnant... According to army records he had no other relatives. Where he came from remains unknown, but as a full blooded Navajo he most likely originated from the Nevada region, but their record keeping there wasn't as thorough as it should have been," Father Andrew finished.

Mrs Willoughby wiped away the tears that flowed down her cheeks, and Yahzi took her hand to comfort her.

Nayati commented. "Your father actions were brave and good. You can be proud, Yiska," he told his brother.

"There are none braver that would give up their own life rather than take another's," Mrs Willoughby added.

Father Andrew asked Yiska to come outside for some air and led him out.

"I hope this is all you need to let this matter rest now Yiska. There is nothing else to discover. You've come from parents that were strong and good and I realize you've inherited many of their traits. Nayati is right; you can feel proud of them! Your mother showed a strength to match your father's in giving you up just before she died. She thought only of you. I will help you contact your mother's friend in Canada if you wish, to find out more about what she was like."

Yiska nodded. "I would like that Father Andrew; I would like that a lot. I cannot begin to tell you how grateful I am for the help you've given me with all this, and Mrs Willoughby."

"You don't need to thank me at all my boy, for you are your parents' son, and I am proud of that too," Father Michael said. "Tell me! Has this changed your mind about what we discussed with Father Michael?" he asked as an afterthought.

"It has made me even more determined, Father Andrew, I can honour them too," he replied.

"I sort of thought it would." Father Andrew said, with resignation.

They sat quietly for a while before returning to Mrs Willoughby's. The old lady discretely concealing the letter while Yiska had been outside.

Father Andrew left for the youth club and Mrs Willoughby decided that she would drop off more clothes, found in her attic, around to Mrs Barlow's for her new guest.

Nayati suggested that they walk to the drive-in to get a burger and fries.

"After all, it is the place where Yahzi and I first met," he said, offering an alternative excuse to the real reason he wanted to go there. As they walked, Nayati brought up the subject of returning home.

"I asked Yahzi to live with us at the cave," he told his brother, eager to hear his thoughts on the matter.

"That is a great idea, Nayati, she will love it there! Niyol will love her as a granddaughter, and Doli as a sister," said Yiska smiling.

Yahzi glowed at his comments but Yiska's mind wandered back to Doli, how he had missed her these past weeks. Nayati noticed his faraway look.

"Doli will be glad to see you also, Brother. You feel about her as I do about Yahzi," he said smiling.

"You are right Brother." Yiska admitted but wasn't feeling like smiling.

Nayati announced that he would like to return home this coming weekend and Yiska nodded his approval.

"Have you noticed that the eagle no longer flies above us, I've not seen it since the day before the track meet?" Yiska asked Nayati.

"I have not seen it either," Nayati told him.

"Does this make you feel uneasy?" Yiska prompted.

"Niyol said that we travel a long and difficult journey. That is why the eagle spirit watches over us. It is my thinking that the difficult days are over, and our journey will now get easier," Nayati answered.

"You are sounding like your grandfather again," Yiska laughed, adding, "That is a good thing."

Nayati grinned at the compliment and told Yiska that, as they only had two days left here, he would like to buy presents for Doli and Niyol. Yiska agreed and thought that with Yahzi's help, they could get Doli something special.

Chapter 31:
Shopping

The following evening, before venturing to the soup kitchen, they told Mrs Willoughby they would be leaving in a few days' time. Devastated at the news, the tears flowed down her cheeks. Yahzi comforted her as best she could, but even that could not stem the sea of tears that swept in like an incoming tide.

"What will I do without you?" she asked, misery etched in her face. "What will Father Andrew do without you?"

"There will be other people for you to help, people who also need the love and care that you showed me," Yahzi told her. "There are many volunteers at the youth club and the soup kitchen now, but few like yourself and Mrs Baker."

"That's true, but it won't be the same without the three of you," said Mrs Willoughby.

"Then it's up to you to make it even better, Mrs Willoughby, and I for one know that you can," said Yiska gently.

"I will try, but you three are a hard act to follow," she said, forcing a smile.

"We come near to here, once or twice a year, to trade for supplies. We will visit you and Father Andrew," Nayati told her.

"Yes do that, and bring your sister and grandfather too, I'd love to meet them!" responded Mrs Willoughby, gaining control of her emotions.

They told Father Andrew at the soup kitchen who nodded and told them he'd guessed that they would return home after Yiska had received the information about his parents. He tried to be his normal, jolly self that evening but couldn't hide his disappointment. They informed the street people who promised a farewell celebration.

On their way home, Nayati told them that he hadn't believed it was possible to become attached to another place and other people in the way they had, and Yiska agreed.

"Do you remember when you made tea for Doli, and I told you it was woman's work, Yiska?" Nayati asked him.

"And do you remember what you told me?" he continued.

Yiska nodded. "It is good to do something for somebody else."

"It is as you say, my Brother. I too, feel good about the work we have done here," Nayati finished.

"I share that feeling," Yiska told him.

The day before leaving, the three of them went shopping. Despite having stayed in Muirfield for some time, they'd scarcely visited the shops. Yahzi, however, showed excitement at the idea and couldn't wait to visit some of the shops whose windows she'd peered many times in her past.

She suggested a dress for Doli, and Nayati thought a new hunting knife for Niyol would be a good idea.

Yahzi led the way to a dress shop that she knew, and the three of them walked in. An assistant immediately came across to offer her services, asking what they were looking for. Nayati produced a winning smile and told her what they required.

Yiska suggested that Yahzi try on dresses, to see how they looked. He explained to the assistant who could not take her eyes off Nayati, that Doli although taller, was of a similar slim build to Yahzi. Yahzi was in her element; she tried on one dress after another, before Yiska chose a dress that matched the striking blue of Nayati and Doli's eyes. They also bought a flowing skirt for Yahzi that had particularly suited her. After paying, they left the shop and continued down the street.

Next, they stopped at a hardware store to study a large display of hunting knives. Yiska wanted to choose a special one for Niyol, as he had given him a particularly fine one belonging to his late brother. Nayati selected one that had a handle carved from the antler of a blackbuck antelope and his brother confirmed the choice.

Something for Mrs Willoughby was more difficult, until Yahzi suggested taking a photograph of the three of them and putting it in a silver-coloured frame. At the end of the block they discovered a photographer capable of taking and developing a picture the same day. He seemed ancient and insisted on showing them a range of formal portraits designed to show off his skill at photographing family groups.

Yiska suggested something less formal would be better, without the forced smiles that dominated the selection the man showed them. He recalled the address confusion with the Deputy Sheriff and as they laughed together again, and the photographer captured their natural smiles. They chose an elegant frame to put it in and paid the photographer before promising to return and pick it up just before closing time that evening.

Their next stop was a small store selling authentic Native American goods, full of the items that Nayati had seen in the trade markets with Niyol.

"Father Michael and Father Andrew are men with big dreams," he told them. "It would be right to give them a dream-catcher, so that they will never lose their dreams."

Yiska loved the idea and helped select two attractive ones from the selection on offer. With their shopping completed, they headed down the street towards the drive-in for Nayati, who knew he would miss the place. They had more than an hour to wait for their photograph to be ready and it would help to pass the time.

After they had eaten, they walked back towards the photographer's. Passing a small shop that displayed a multitude of items in its windows, old and used; Yiska asked Yahzi what sort of shop it was, and she explained the concept behind a pawn-broker. Yiska suddenly froze, not hearing what Yahzi was saying. His brother noticed the colour drained from his face.

"What is it Brother? What is wrong?" Nayati asked, worried.

Yiska did not respond to Nayati's questions and Nayati thought that perhaps his brother was getting another flashback from his troubled past. In desperation Nayati shook him by the shoulders and watched carefully as his brother regained his senses.

"What is it?" he asked again.

Yiska raised his arm and pointed to a box that sat on the bottom of the three shelves. His arm was shaking.

"The box!" he said, his voice trembling.

Nayati suddenly realised the significance. "It is your box?" he asked incredulously.

"Yes, no, I mean maybe. It's the same, but has a piece broken off the corner of the lid," he said, the words rushing out at twice the normal speed. "I need to see it," and with that, he marched into the shop, Nayati and Yahzi following behind.

A middle-aged man approached them as they entered. "What can I do for you?" he asked, his face breaking into a well-practised, but false, smile.

"The box, in the window, how long have you owned it?" Yiska asked, pointing to it.

"Years now. Nobody wants it because of the broken corner. Should have thrown it away, but I paid for it once and... Well, you never know, somebody might want it!" the shopkeeper told him.

"Do you remember who you bought it from?" asked Yiska.

"No, it was too long ago. But it had a few items inside it, if I remember right."

"Some war medals and a St. Christopher?" Yiska urged.

"Do you know? I think you are right! They're not in it now though; those sell well, probably gone long ago. How do you know?" he asked, curiosity building.

"How much is the box?" Yiska asked.

There was a label attached to the box, and the shopkeeper read out the price. "Two dollars," he said. Yiska paid for it and the three of them left the shop.

"Is it your box?" Nayati asked gently.

"I'll know in just a minute," said Yiska and started leading the way towards the track, just a short walk away.

When they reached it, Yiska sat on the ground and crossed his legs.

"My box had a split in the lining at one end and I used to keep a letter hidden underneath it. If the box also has this, then it must be my box. If not, I have a box to remind me of the one taken from me."

It infected Yahzi with a sudden sense of urgency.

"Open it, Yiska!" she said. So Yiska lifted the lid.

The lining was the same colour as the one he remembered. He ran his fingers along the lining and pulled it gently at the end, it lifted away from the box.

Yahzi squealed as she saw a glimpse of the ageing envelope that still lay hidden below.

"The letter is still there!" she said.

Yiska carefully withdrew the envelope, opened it and unfolded the sheet of paper that lay within. He looked at the beautiful writing and a single tear slid down his cheek.

"I thought I lost this forever," he said in a quiet voice.

"Can you read it?"

"I can read some words, but the writing makes it look strange. I do not think I will understand all the words," Yahzi answered.

"It's not a problem, I will ask Mrs Willoughby to read it to us later," Yiska replied, returning the sheet to its envelope.

He placed it back in its secret place in the box, closing the lid gently. He held it close to his body.

"This was my mother's and now I own something of hers!" he said, smiling.

They collected the photograph and frame on their way back to Mrs Willoughby's, where Yahzi explained what had happened.

"My goodness, what an amazing stroke of luck," she said, in astonishment, "And the Lord knows that you deserve that! Would you like me to read it to you, Yiska?"

In silence, he handed her the envelope and sank down onto the couch, gazing at her in anticipation. She sat down next to him, gestured to the others to do likewise and opened the letter.

My darling boy,

You've given me so much joy these past few years, that it makes this letter seem inadequate. There is so much that I'd like to share with you, but my illness has drained me of strength. I've so little time left…

I discovered a fine place to take you, an orphanage where the people seem devoted to the children. When you're older, you'll understand that leaving you somewhere safe was my last gift to you. I could not bear to die, and have you taken by strangers.

You never had the chance to meet your father, but I want you to know he was a good and decent man. You already have his patience and serenity; I hope that you will grow up to be as fine a man as he was.

I've bequeathed you a box, made by your father as a gift to me–he was so clever with his hands. This box and its contents are the only possessions of value I have, not monetary value, just sentimental value; medication for this horrible disease has forced me to sell just about everything else.

Your grandmother gave me the St. Christopher as a gift before she died, many years ago and it seems quite fitting that I pass it on to you.

Last, the medals are your father's, for saving the lives of his comrades. He hated the war and fighting but had no choice. Even though he went, he vowed not to take a life. From what I've heard since, he achieved this; even though his actions led to his own death."

Knowing that I'm leaving you alone in the world is the most awful thought that will haunt me forever, but I am fortunate that my day of reckoning is not far away. I love you, my son, more than I could ever say. I wish I had more to leave you; I wish I could witness you grow up; so many things to wish for.

Make a good life for yourself, listen to those around you that offer you knowledge and wisdom. And above all–be true to yourself. God bless you, son.

All my love forever and a day,
Mommy

Mrs Willoughby folded the letter, placed it back in the envelope and handed it to Yiska, who took it silently from her. She then wiped the tears from her face and stood up to fetch a glass of water. Nobody said a word, and a silent atmosphere prevailed. When she returned, she sat back down.

"Your mother was a very brave woman, Yiska," she said. "It's incredibly brave for a woman to give away her son before she died. She couldn't know the true nature of that orphanage. All this after losing her husband in the war! I think you can be very proud of both of your parents; just as they would be proud of you, if they were alive today. I believe that you're already doing the things that your mother asks of you. You honour them!"
Yiska nodded his thanks but remained silent.

Their last evening at the soup kitchen passed by quickly, despite their staying long after it closed. Enthusiastic farewells and good wishes prevailed with promises made to revisit when they came to town in the future.

By normal standards, Yiska was subdued, and Nayati and Yahzi both tried to help him feel better, forcing him to join in many conversations that he might otherwise avoid.

On their return to Mrs Willoughby's, Nayati asked what was troubling him, but Yiska fended him off, saying he needed to think. Nayati tried again, reminding him that he would see Doli soon, but again, Yiska said nothing in reply.

Chapter 32:
The Parting

The morning of their departure arrived and the three of them collected their belongings and placed them by the front door. It was amazing how few belongings they owned, more than they'd arrived with though.

Mrs Willoughby had made them a final, cooked breakfast to help with the long journey that lay ahead of them. They helped her clear away, before announcing that it was time to leave.

Yahzi handed her the gift they'd bought for her, which she opened. The gesture surprised her; it had been a long while since anybody had bought her anything. She loved the photograph and its frame and immediately placed it above the fire. Then she announced that she had something for them and gave them each a small wrapped box. Yiska opened his first to find a silver St. Christopher on a chain.

"I know that it can't replace the one given to you by your mother, but St. Christopher is the patron saint of travellers, and your journey still continues. Wear it and think of me, sometimes!" she said to Yiska, taking it from him and fastening it round his neck. "There's one here for Doli too, she said handing him a second box.

Nayati and Yahzi opened their packages, to find the same gift which she also put around their necks for them.

"Mrs Willoughby, I don't have the words to thank you for what you've done for us. You are a very special person and I'm proud to have you as my friend," said Yiska, as he stooped to give the woman a hug and a kiss on the cheek.

Nayati and Yahzi added farewells, and they left the house for the last time.

As they walked towards the end of the street, Father Andrew rounded the corner.

"I've just come to say goodbye and thank you again for all the hard work you've done here," he told them. "I want you to know that you've more friends here than perhaps you realise, and to hold you to the promise you made to visit when you go to one of your trade fairs."

"We will honour our promise," Nayati told him.

Yahzi presented him with the gift they'd bought for him and told him to keep dreaming big. The present touched Father Andrew, and they noticed his eyes moistening.

"Be off with you, then!" he said, and waved to them as they walked away.

Yiska told them that they'd could collect their belongings that still lay hidden outside town and travel straight on to Mason. They would camp where he and Nayati had camped before and visit Father Michael tonight. Then they could begin their journey home tomorrow.

As they uncovered their belongings, it surprised Yahzi to see bows and arrows.

"My goodness it's a good job you didn't bring those into town; they would have arrested you!" she told them.

"We did not know where we would stay and how we would eat," Nayati told her. "These are tools we use to catch food. Our life is different in the mountains."

Yiska nodded in agreement. "There is a lot to learn, but I promise you there are no better teachers than Niyol, Nayati and Doli."

"I am so excited by all this; I can't wait to get started!" Yahzi told them.

They arrived at their campsite outside Mason just as the sun was setting. Nayati announced that his hunger was making sounds in his stomach, so they set out to find the diner.

"It will be the last time you'll taste this food for a while," Yiska told Nayati.

"That's true! But I will bring Niyol here when we travel to trade. It is my thinking he will like this," he said, grinning.

After eating their fill, they made their way to the youth club to say goodbye to Father Michael. They found him playing table tennis with some of the children and losing. Pleased for an excuse to stop, their thoughtful gift touched him and said that it would remind him of them whenever he looked at it.

Nayati introduced Yahzi to some of the children that they had befriended during the time they had stayed here, whilst Father Michael and Yiska sat in a corner, deep in conversation. When the youth club shut for the evening, Nayati and Yahzi bade their farewells to Father Michael. Yiska shook his hand and said something to him that the others couldn't hear. Then they returned to the campsite to rest for the day's travel ahead, but sleep did not come easy for Yiska.

As was their custom, they awoke as the first light of day extended across the darkened sky. Nayati couldn't hide his excitement at the prospect of going home.

"Soon you will meet Doli," he told his brother. Yiska didn't answer but, sadness extended across his face.

"What troubles you?" asked Nayati, noticing the look.

"We need to talk, Nayati. There is something I need to tell you, it isn't easy," said Yiska, Nayati held his brother's eyes and again read the sadness there.

"What is it?" he asked again.

"Today, you and Yahzi travel alone, for I cannot return to our home yet," Yiska told him.

Nayati stared at him in disbelief.

"What do you mean by this? We are always together, this is how it is!" he said, incredulously.

"I cannot return home yet. I must stay," explained Yiska.

"What is so important that it keeps us apart?" persisted Nayati.

Yiska sat down and motioned Nayati and Yahzi to do the same.

"For a while our journeys must take different paths. You must take Yahzi home and help her adjust to the ways of our life. My journey here is unfinished. I've dishonoured my parents, you, Niyol and Doli in the actions I took at the orphanage. I helped them steal from people's homes. You would not do this; Niyol and Doli would not do this. My father went to war and refused to take another's life. My actions show my dishonour," he said.

"This is not so, my Brother, for you did not do as they asked, and they beat you for it. You suffered because you did the right thing. You were too young to know different, at the start. No man can blame you," Nayati tried to reason.

"I cannot hide the shame I feel, and the wrong I did. I've dishonoured the people I care most about. Nothing can change how I feel," answered Yiska.

"What will you do? Where will you stay?" asked Nayati.

"I've spoken with Father Andrew and Father Michael and told them that I must pay for the things I did. It's agreed that I will remain in Mason for one year and help to start up a soup kitchen like the one in Muirfield. I will stay with Father Michael, then I will return home to you, Doli, Niyol and Yahzi when I've finished," Yiska told him.

"I will bring Doli to you when we trade," offered Nayati.

"No, this is to be my punishment. I will not be worthy of Doli until I've done this. I can't let her see my shame," Yiska replied.

Nayati changed tack. "I can no longer imagine life without you; you are like my hand, joined to me. There must be another way."

"There is no other way! Ask Yahzi, she has paid for what she did, and she understands how I feel."

Nayati looked at Yahzi for help, but the response wasn't what he wanted.

"He is right, Nayati, in what he says. The guilt I had, weighed heavy in my thoughts. It takes time to heal the wounds. I took three years to find peace. Yiska's actions were less than mine and he has said one year to repay what he has done. It's fair, and I hope it is enough. Don't talk him out of this Nayati because he will never be his old self with the knowledge he carries around," she said.

"I am saddened by this, but it will be as you say," Nayati told Yiska. "Know this Brother. To my thinking, you did no wrong, I am not dishonoured by you; my life is better for having you in it. I am proud to be your brother."

"I will spend this time in Mason, and then I will return. We will be as we once were, and I will be as proud to be your brother as I am proud to have you as mine," said Yiska.

The conversation ended and Yiska helped them pack up their things. He asked them to take his possessions back to the cave, as he believed he wouldn't need them here.

Nayati told him that he would visit Mason and Muirfield during the time of the trading, to visit with their friends but he would not seek Yiska out.

"I will keep all my promises," he told his brother.

From above the cry of an eagle broke their discussion as they looked up.

"The eagle has returned to guide you home, Nayati," Yiska told him, pleased to see the bird again. He hugged his brother and told him to travel well. Then he hugged Yahzi and kissed her gently on her cheek.

"Tell Doli that I miss her and that I will return to her. Explain to her my reasons for you really understand them. Look after Nayati and listen well to Niyol," he said.

She nodded. "You take good care of yourself too, and I will see you in one year. Or we will come to get you!" she told him.

He watched as they slowly walked away from him.

Yahzi turned her head. "Good luck, Yiska!" she said.

Yiska responded. "You too, Yahzi."

Nayati's shoulders hung lower as the distance between him and his brother increased. A single tear fell down his cheek. Yahzi took his hand, but he made no attempt to wipe it away. He turned one last time, making out the silhouette of his brother. He stopped and cupped his hands to his mouth.

"I see you Yiska, you are my brother as I am yours. It will always be as I say," he yelled.

A moment passed, and the response carried on the breeze.

"It is as you say Brother."

C. S. Clifford has always been passionate about stories and storytelling. As a child he earned money singing at weddings in the church choir; the proceeds of which were spent in the local bookshop.

As a former primary teacher, he was inspired to start writing through the constant requests of the children he taught. He lives in Kent where, when not writing or promoting and teaching writing, he enjoys carpentry, sea and freshwater angling and exploring the history of his local countryside.